First Came the Owl

First Came the Owl

Judy Richardson

Judith Benét Richardson

Henry Holt and Company · New York

Henry Holt and Company, Inc., *Publishers since 1866*
115 West 18th Street, New York, New York 10011
Henry Holt is a registered trademark of Henry Holt and Company, Inc.
Copyright © 1996 by Judith Benét Richardson
All rights reserved.
Published in Canada by Fitzhenry & Whiteside Ltd.,
195 Allstate Parkway, Markham, Ontario L3R 4T8.

Library of Congress Cataloging-in-Publication Data
Richardson, Judith Benét.
First came the owl / Judith Benét Richardson.
p.   cm.
Summary: Shy eleven-year-old Nita feels lost when her mother returns
from a visit to their home country, Thailand, and plunges into depression, but
with the help of friends, a school play, and the appearance of a special visitor,
Nita begins to blossom and her shyness disappears.
[1. Self-confidence—Fiction.   2. Depression, Mental—Fiction.
3. Mothers and daughters—Fiction.   4. Amerasians—Fiction.]   I. Title.
PZ7.R3949Fi   1996   [Fic]—dc20   95-46286

ISBN 0-8050-4547-3
First Edition—1996
Printed in the United States of America on acid-free paper.   ∞
1   3   5   7   9   10   8   6   4   2

For my great(terrific!)-nieces:
Francesca
Elizabeth
Lucy
Isabel
and
Anita Jane

First Came the Owl

One

"HENRY SPORONI says I look like a monkey," said Nita.

Her mother lay on the bed facing the wall. The wall was made of wood strips painted with shiny varnish. Nita's mother had picked the varnish off the part of the wall she stared at as she lay there under the white chenille bedspread.

"I told Henry Sporoni *he* looked like a rat." Nita wriggled her nose like a rat, hoping her mother would turn over and look.

Nothing happened. Nita went into the living room and pressed her face against the cold window. Frost decorated the window in feathery stars of ice. It was a dark morning, and the lighthouse flashed even though it was day. Flash! And then dark. Flash! And then dark. Nita loved living in the Coast Guard house right next to the big light, but now even the steady pulse of the beam was no comfort. I *wish* I had told Henry Sporoni he looked like a rat, thought Nita.

"Nita, I packed your lunch," said Dad, coming out of the kitchen. "It's on the counter." He took his parka off the coatrack and put it over his Coast Guard uniform. "I've got to run now, but I'll be back here at lunchtime."

As if everything were just fine, thought Nita. "But what about Mom?" she asked him. "Won't she get up?" Mom, who usually watered her orchids and sang and cooked spicy noodles, lay on her bed in the other room and had hardly talked at all for two whole days.

Dad opened the door and a freezing draft of air rushed in. He looked at his watch. "Eight bells! I'll be back in a few hours, and I'll figure out . . . something. Try not to worry, Nita." His blue eyes crinkled in a smile.

"Aye, aye, sir!" Nita said, and tried to smile back. The door slammed behind Dad, and Nita heard his car start up.

The house seemed so empty. Nita tiptoed over to the bedroom door and peeked in. Mom's small form humped up the white bedspread and lay perfectly still. It was almost as if Nita were alone in the house.

When Mom first came back from her trip to Thailand last month, she was fine. Even though she'd had to travel quickly for her grandmother's funeral, she'd seen all of her family, and she told Nita about her cousins and brought her a beautiful shirt with elephants on it to wear. Then she got quieter and quieter and stayed in bed more and more. Nita knew Mom had been to the doctor and had some pills to take. "For depression," Dad said. That was the first time Nita knew you could take pills for being sad. But now it seemed like Mom was sadder.

Nita went back to the window. She looked out at the snowy world etched in white and gray. Only the waves moved this morning, clawing at the shore. The rest of the world was a black-and-white photograph, frozen in place. There weren't even any birds on the feeder.

It's different from Thailand, that's for sure, thought Nita. I remember palm trees and rice fields and dark wood buildings, and it was warm. But the faces of people who must have been Mom's family are blurry. I guess I don't remember much about Thailand. I positively don't remember when Mom and Dad got married. How could I? I wasn't even born.

I remember some of the other Coast Guard bases we've lived on, but Maushope's Landing is the farthest north we've ever been. This is the first place we've ever had snow.

"I have to go to school, Mom," called Nita to the still figure in the other room. There was no answer, but maybe Mom was asleep. Nita picked up the pot of yellow dancing lady orchids and put it on the table just inside the bedroom door.

Then she put on her jacket, her mittens, and her bunny fur earmuffs. She got her lunch from the kitchen. "Bye, Mom," she called again, as if by doing everything exactly the way she always did, it would somehow make Mom the way she used to be.

Then Nita was out in the frosty air. She picked her way down the icy path and headed along the beach road toward town. The waves lapped at the narrow beach. Just as Nita tucked her chin down in her collar, she thought she saw a sudden movement out of the corner of her eye. What was it? A piece of sand dune seemed to fly up, and a white flash of something big caught Nita's glance. Was it a bird? If that was a bird, it was sure a big one, she thought. It was gone before she could really tell what she had seen, but the surprise of the dazzling whiteness stayed with her all the way to the end of the road.

Nita took the shortcut through the ferry parking lot, up behind the post office, and across the street to School Street. In Maushope's Landing, the school was on School Street, the church was on Church Street, and the main street was Water Street because it ran along the water.

The old wooden school came into view, and Nita ran a few steps because she was so glad to be there. School is safe, school is always the same, thought Nita. Even the desks have been there for about a hundred years. "Good morning," Nita heard someone say.

Nita whirled around. There was her teacher. Mrs. Sommers' arms were full. Her grayish-brown hair wisped out from under a shapeless brown hat. As she spoke, a folder of math papers slipped to the ground. Nita rushed to pick it up.

"Hi," she said softly. When Mrs. Sommers went up to the classroom, Nita was alone again, but it was nice to be the very first person on the playground. A seagull flew over. The sky was lighter now, and this morning's few snowflakes hadn't covered the *Run, Sheep, Run* tracks in what was left of last week's snow on the playground.

A yellow school bus roared up School Street, its brakes screeching as it stopped by the gate. Noise and color burst into the gray and white world and a wave of kids flowed onto the playground. For a second Nita wanted to run inside and hide in the closet, but then she was swept up in the wave.

"The Sporoni bus is here," shouted Henry. He hopped up on the low stone wall at the edge of the playground and pretended to play a trumpet fanfare to celebrate his arrival. "Ta-da! Ta-da-da-da-a!"

Nita edged away from Henry and her eyes searched the crowd for Anne, her best friend since the second day of the fourth grade, the year Nita had arrived in Maushope's Landing. They both had dark brown, almost black, eyes, and they laughed at the same jokes. And they were *quiet*, not like some noisy people—for instance, someone with the initials H.S.

The first bell had already rung when Anne ran down the sidewalk and through the gate into the school yard. She squeezed into line with Nita, ignoring the glares of Brenda, who knew perfectly well that Nita always saved a place for Anne. "I don't want to miss the tryouts," she said breathlessly. Anne's socks were two different shades of blue and the sweatshirt that showed under her yellow jacket was on backward, but Nita always thought Anne looked great. She almost danced when she walked. Now she smiled at Nita.

"Oh, I forgot about *Snow White*," said Nita. "But . . . I don't think I could be in a play."

Brenda had overheard them. *"I'm* going to be in the play. I love acting." She tossed her long red hair back and posed with her arms out and her mouth open.

Nita wanted to be in the play if Anne was in it, but what if she opened her mouth and no words came out? What if she tripped? What if . . .

The second bell rang, and the fifth- and sixth-grade class trampled up the stairs.

"Let's go skating after school," said Pete.

"I'd rather try out for Amy's play," said Anne, putting her books on her desk.

Henry *stood* on his desk. "Too many girls," said Henry, as he surveyed the class from on high. "That's the only trouble with the fifth grade. Too many girls. Now they want to have some baby play."

"Henry, get off your desk, please," said Mrs. Sommers. Honestly, thought Nita, she would say "please" if Henry were about to light a string of firecrackers right there in the classroom. "And Anne, you can try out for the play after school the day after tomorrow," the teacher went on, "though I'm not sure some people in this class are mature enough to manage a whole play on their own."

"Amy will manage them," said Anne, frowning at Henry. "It's going to be the Maushope's Landing fifth-grade play, and it's not a baby play, it's a 'timeless classic,' that's what Amy says, and it'll be the best play we've ever had!"

Nita knew Amy Bradley a little bit because her house was near the lighthouse, but Amy was in the eighth grade. She took a bus up to Maushop to the junior high instead of coming to the Landing school.

"Well, right now I want to hear about your reports," said Mrs. Sommers. "They've got to be done, too, play or no play."

Oh no, thought Nita. I still don't know what to do my report on.

"I'm going to do my report on stones," said Anne.

"I'm going to do my report on bones," said Pete. Everyone laughed, but his father *was* an archaeologist, when he wasn't a fisherman.

Even though she was still worried about her report, Nita sank into her school mood at last. She savored the neat writing on the blackboard, the tick of the clock, and doing the same things every day—that you could count on. Now she watched Mrs. Sommers writing her report list on the blackboard in her beautiful cursive writing.

Nita leaned sideways to see what Anne was writing

in her notebook. It wasn't her report. She wrote: Snow White sleeps a long time. Maybe frozen? Like winter? Then Anne drew in her notebook. It was winter. The sun set behind a sort of box with a girl inside. "Snow White in the glass coffin," Anne whispered when she saw Nita watching.

This sounded like a sad play. Nita wasn't sure she wanted anything to do with it.

"Nita?" said Mrs. Sommers.

"What?" Nita answered, startled.

"Your report? Have you decided?"

"Uh, not yet."

"Well, please decide today, so we can talk it over," said Mrs. Sommers. She pushed a loose hairpin back into her bun. Sometimes she seemed distracted, but she *always* remembered to ask about things like this darn report.

"It doesn't matter what you decide," said Mrs. Sommers. "This is your library report, to prove you can look up absolutely anything in the library."

"Even outer space aliens from the planet Sporoni?"

"Even tuna fish sandwiches?"

"All right, class," said their teacher. "It's a little early, but you sound like you need your recess. *Slowly* on the stairs now."

The class pounded down the stairs to the front

door, not running exactly, but letting their feet thud extra hard. Henry stepped on his sneaker laces and fell down the two outside steps onto the playground.

It was cold on the playground, almost too cold to snow. Nita put on her earmuffs and shivered.

"Come on, Nita," said Anne and ran into the *Run, Sheep, Run* circle. Nita just couldn't step inside that running pack. Instead she climbed to the top of the monkey bars and watched Henry finish tying his sneaker laces.

As he finished, she looked away, but not before he saw her watching. Henry stayed crouched on the ground, scratched under his arms, and cried, "Chee, chee, chee." He bounced sideways and scraped the backs of his hands along the ground in an apelike way. Nita was afraid to eat the banana she had brought for her snack, because then Henry would really go crazy. I never should have climbed these monkey bars, either, she thought.

She wriggled her nose at Henry, but she was so far away, he probably didn't notice. "Rat," she said softly. Henry's nose *was* kind of pointed, and he did stick it into everything. Maybe he could find some rat bars to climb.

She looked at the sun. The sun was white and shiny

in the gray winter sky. It looks like my hard-boiled egg when I peel it at lunchtime, thought Nita. It doesn't feel warm at all. She was getting hungry. Was Henry gone? He was in the sheep circle now. Nita turned her back on the game and sneaked her banana out of her pocket.

Across the pond she could see the back of the laboratory where Anne's parents were busy in their geology lab. Nita wished her mother would go to an office or a lab, or water her orchids or *something*. Everyone is busy with something, except Mom. She thought of her mother lying on her bed. Even though we've moved around a lot, she argued to herself, we were always the Orson family, we were always fine, and now . . . now we're not fine.

She turned back and looked down from the monkey bars at Anne and Henry, Pete and Brenda, in the snowy circle. Brenda was the fastest sheep, with her long, red hair streaming behind her. Henry was the wolf, of course. The rat-wolf.

They all seemed far away from Nita's perch high up on the monkey bars. When she was in school, she liked to *be* in school; when she was at home, she liked to be there with her Mom and Dad, the way things had always been.

"Time to go," shouted the bell monitor. He swung

the big hand bell. Kids jostled toward the door and pushed into line. Nita made her way slowly to the lineup, but she felt as though she were invisible, because Henry trampled right over her foot and Anne was talking with Brenda. They were talking about the play.

Two

"NITA!" Back in the classroom, Anne leaned over the back of Nita's seat and looked at her as if a question needed to be answered. "*Please* be in the play! It will be so fun if we're both in it."

"What could I be?" asked Nita cautiously. After all, the tryouts weren't until day after tomorrow. It wouldn't hurt to ask about the play a little bit.

"We could both be dwarfs. They wear red hats and sing and dance!" Anne's eyes sparkled at Nita.

"I can't dance."

"Also, the dwarfs take care of Snow White," said Anne.

"I can do that," said Nita, thinking of her mother.

"Also, dwarfs are *boys*," said Henry, bursting in on the conversation from his seat across the aisle.

"Well, there must be *some* girl dwarfs," said Anne.

"There aren't," said Henry. "Dwarfs are miners."

"Well, what about baby dwarfs? There must be some mothers."

Henry's face turned red and he pulled his head down into his shirt so he looked like a shirt with hair. He was quiet for one whole minute. Then he gradually sat up, coming out of his shirt like a turtle. When he saw Nita watching him, he made little claws with his hands. "I'm a dwarf," he said menacingly. "Now I'm coming to gobble you up!"

He must mean a troll, Nita thought. Even though she knew it was stupid, his claws made her shiver.

"Boys and girls," said Mrs. Sommers. "I want to give you back these math tests. What a debacle!"

Somebody started to say, "What does . . . ?"

"Look it up in your dictionaries," chorused at least twenty voices. Mrs. Sommers always said this, and today the class beat her to it.

The day sped on. Math, lunch, it seemed to Nita to go faster as it got toward the end and she knew she would have to go home. Pete got some people to go skating, but Nita didn't have her skates. The Sporoni bus picked up its passengers and left, with Henry sitting quietly in a front seat. His mother was the bus driver, and the only known human who was able to control Henry.

Nita dragged her feet as she went down School Street. She didn't feel like going home. It would be too quiet and scary.

Water Street was nice, and she slowed down to enjoy it. The post office had evergreen wreaths and fake candles in the windows, and she knew she could go in and have a gumdrop. Even grownups ate them, so they could joke around with John the Postmaster. But Nita didn't feel up to joking.

The bookstore was bright with the shiny covers of new books, and the other store in the bookstore building had a golden sun right in its window. Nita looked at the real sky, with only a pale gray glare where the sun should be. The one in the store window was *much* better. Up close, Nita could see it was made of little bits of fabric, a quilted sun. She smiled back at the glowing window.

Suddenly, Brenda came flying around the corner. "Race you to the bike path," she shouted. Nita started running without thinking, and she almost caught her. "Last one there is a rotten egg!" shouted Brenda. Nita sped up and just managed to tag the back of Brenda's jacket as she ran through the ferry parking lot gate and took off up the bike path. Not too rotten, Nita said to herself.

Now she was farther toward home. She walked slowly under the railroad bridge, staying on the side that had no pigeons cooing in the beams.

It will be fine, it will be okay, Dad will be home soon, but why is Mom so sad? Nita walked and worried up the shortcut, down the street and all the way down the beach, up the driveway, and into the white house by the lighthouse whose light was flashing out over the bay.

Warning! Rocks and shoals! Warning! flashed the big light.

Three

CRACK! Nita cracked an egg on the side of the bowl. It looked fine. What was a rotten egg? she wondered. Her mind went back to the race with Brenda.

"What's a rotten egg like?" she asked her father.

"Sulfur." He bent down and sniffed the bowl. "But those eggs aren't rotten. They'd smell like sulfur. Like the fires of hell."

Nita laughed. Her father had fancy ways of saying things. Boy, sulfur must be awful. But she was tired of eggs—an egg for lunch, and now, eggs for dinner. No one was doing the shopping, that's why.

Dad smiled at Nita, and his blue eyes creased around

the edges. It always surprised Nita that she could have such a blue-eyed dad. He had explained to her about genes and blue eyes, how if one parent had brown eyes and no gene for blue eyes that the children would always have brown eyes. But it wasn't only that. Nita *looked* like her mother, dark eyes, black hair, brown skin. Her father was pale skinned and blue eyed and looked like what Nita thought of as American. She didn't think she looked half American, though Dad said she had inherited his stubborn look and his love of potato chips.

Now she beat the eggs with a fork. "I'm going to cook them. You could get Mom."

Nita heard him in the other room, coaxing Mom. She put some bean sprouts and green onions into the egg mixture and dropped little egg pancakes into the sizzling pan. The rice was done.

When Mom came to the table she was quiet. She looks so mysterious, thought Nita. What is she thinking? Her smooth brown face didn't give away her thoughts. Mom was sealed off like someone in a space capsule going to the moon. Earth to Mom, thought Nita. Talk to me. Why won't she talk to me? Nita felt so lonely right there next to her mother with Silence sitting like a fourth person at the table.

She put her mother's plate down in front of her.

Dad tried to keep the conversation going, but it was hard to talk to Silence. So he turned to Nita.

"How was school?"

"It was . . . school-like. Oh, and there's going to be a play—*Snow White and the Seven Dwarfs*."

Mom didn't pick up her fork. Dad cut a little bite and tried to put the fork in her hand. Nita knew he hated to feed Mom because he felt she wouldn't like being treated like a baby. Tonight Mom just shook her head.

Nita tried again. "I saw something on my way to school—I think it was a big bird, and it wasn't a seagull."

No one seemed to be listening. Nita felt a burst of anger in her chest, but she knew that wasn't fair. Dad had explained to her about depression. She can't help it, he said. But it would be so easy to just pick up that fork and *eat*! Nita knew Dad would be unhappy if she said that, so she stuffed her mouth with egg and finished her supper quickly.

Then she took the phone into her room.

"Hello, is Anne there?" She hoped Dad wasn't listening. He thought she should say, "Hello, this is Nita. May I please speak to Anne?" But *no* one said all that, especially when it was Anne's sister Petrova who answered. Nita was sure Petrova didn't like her. She was so abrupt.

"Hold on," said Petrova, and dropped the phone, or at least that's how it sounded.

"Listen, I can't talk long," said Anne. "My parents are 'helping' me with my math." Anne's parents and her sister were all very good at math, and they couldn't believe that Anne wasn't. So they "helped" her, it seemed like for hours, when they weren't too busy. Fortunately, that wasn't very often.

Dad poked his head around the door, looking serious. "Nita, I need to use the phone," he said. "Will you go sit with Mom? In fact, is that Anne? Ask her if I can talk to her mother, will you?"

All these questions. Silently, Nita handed him the phone and let him ask for Anne's mother. Then he gestured at Nita, to shoo her out the door, and reluctantly, she went. It was her room, after all, and what were they going to talk about anyway? Why did he want to talk to Mrs. S.? Now Nita was the one with all the questions. As she dawdled out of the room, she heard him say, "I'm going to ask you a big favor, Marian."

Mom was back on her bed. She lay on her side facing the wood-paneled wall and pick, picked at the varnish. Long shreds of wood were coming off, and as Nita looked closer, she saw there was blood on the tips of her mother's fingers. Nita took her mother's hand. There was a big splinter in one finger. Her mother rolled onto her back and her dark eyes looked past Nita to the window.

Carefully, Nita laid down the hand and whispered, "I'll be right back. I'll fix it." She hurried into the kitchen and got the splinter needle that was stuck in the bulletin board by the phone. She lit the stove and sterilized the tip of the needle in the flame. Then she went back to the bedroom and sat on the edge of the bed.

Gently, Nita picked up her mother's hand again. It was practically no bigger than Nita's own hand, and soft. Nita picked at the splinter. She was afraid it might hurt, but Mom didn't seem to even feel it. There! The splinter eased out. It *was* out. But a big drop of blood came out after it, and dropped on the bedspread.

Tears rushed to Nita's eyes. "Mom!" she burst out. "I'm sorry!" She tried to hug her mother. To do this she had to kneel on the floor and squeeze Mom's shoulders. Mom was so thin. She didn't answer Nita, but she looked at the spot of blood on the white bedspread.

Mom had slipped away into another world, like the fairy-tale world where princesses slept for a hundred years or queens wished for daughters as white as snow, as red as blood, and as black as ebony. She was far away and Nita couldn't think of any way to get to her there.

Nita rested her forehead on the bedspread and her tears dripped onto Mom's silky black hair.

"Nita," said Dad from the doorway. "Nita, come in here for a minute."

Nita left the still figure on the bed and followed Dad into the living room. When he put his arm around her, she leaned against him and wiped her eyes on his shirt.

"I'm going to take her to the hospital," he said. "Anne's mother says you can stay with them tonight. Okay?"

"It's—" Nita was going to say, *not* okay. She didn't like to stay overnight at other people's houses, even Anne's. But Dad looked so worried that she heard herself say, "Okay. Can they . . . can the hospital get her to feel better?"

"They have some different medication, they have things they can try."

"But why won't she talk?"

"She can't," said Dad.

"Is there something the matter with her throat?" Nita asked.

"No."

"Then she *can* talk."

"She can't." Dad spread his hands out by his sides, as if he didn't know what to do. "Nita, I know you're upset. But remember, Mom's had a hard life, and I think her trip reminded her of some sad things."

[24]

Nita did remember one of Mom's stories. A story told long ago, in whispers, of a long escape through the trees, a dark night, and a hunt. Soldiers hunting her mother's family, who ran and ran through the jungle.

But now, Mom wouldn't even tell stories. She was like a clock not working—running down, ticking slower and slower, and finally not working. As if the whole world could just stop. Somehow, Nita felt if Mom would say one word, only one word, the world wouldn't stop. But Mom couldn't.

"Pack some stuff," Dad said. "Marian is coming to get you. I'll call you tomorrow."

He's not looking at me, thought Nita. All he thinks about is her, her, her. Or maybe . . . he's afraid, too? That was the worst thought of all.

Dad gave her another hug, but she could hardly hug him back. Headlights swept the lawn in front of the lighthouse. "Here they are. Get your toothbrush."

Nita hurried into her bedroom and threw some stuff in her duffel bag. Pajamas. Her old stuffed cat. Her school bag and her special pen with a tiny *Mayflower* that sailed back and forth in a capsule of fluid. She put on her earmuffs.

As she went to the front door, she looked back and saw Dad sitting on the edge of Mom's bed. He sat very still, and he didn't turn his head to see Nita leave. She made her way down the path by the flashing lighthouse beam that made things look white and then dark, white and then dark.

Anne gave Nita a scared look when she got into the warm car, but Anne's mother just acted normal.

"Get your skates," said Mrs. S. "Our pond is perfect at the moment, and we're going to go skating by moonlight."

"Tonight?" said Anne and Nita at the same moment.

"Tonight."

Nita smiled thankfully at the back of Mrs. Stillwater's head. She climbed out of the car, went up the slippery path again, and took her skates off the hook by the entryway. She took a last look at her parents through the little window beside the inside door. They hadn't moved.

In the car, Anne bounced on the seat. "Night skating!" she said.

Four

PONDS DIDN'T STAY frozen very long in Maushope's Landing, and tonight there was a moon, but it was also a school night, and even the lively Stillwaters didn't usually let you go out then.

The car went over the hill to High Street. "I'll be right back with some cocoa," said Mrs. S. She went into the house.

"I didn't even know we were going," said Anne. "I think she just thought of it to cheer you up." They got Anne's skates from the bench in her front hall and went back outside.

The moon was out, riding across the sky behind

tattered shreds of cloud. The white blanket of snow in the yard glittered in the moonlight.

When the girls slid down to the pond in back of the house, they saw that the ice was perfect, glassy and smooth. The moon was so bright they could even see the leaves and twigs frozen under the black ice and the moon's reflected light, as if the pond were a mirror.

Nita sat on a log and laced up her skates, then stuffed her hands quickly back into her mittens. She stumbled out onto the ice. "I've forgotten how," she called. She slipped and came down on her hands, but after she got up it began to get easier. She made it all around the edge of the pond and back to Anne, ducking under branches that stuck out over the ice.

"Be my partner," said Anne. They crossed their arms and skated together like performers.

Mrs. Stillwater came down and put the thermos near their shoes by the log. Then she glided onto the ice. She was really good—she could skate backward and twirl.

Around and around they went until Nita felt warm all over. The frozen pond and the moon were cold and beautiful, chilling and exciting at the same time.

"You'll see," said Mrs. S., as she pushed Nita by the arms to help her learn to skate backward. "Your mother will get better. It's as if your Mom has fallen through the ice, but she'll be rescued in time, I really believe that. I know her doctor, she's a good doctor."

Nita couldn't answer. It was the first time anyone but Dad had ever talked to her about Mom. It felt embarrassing but good, good to be out of the lonely house by the lighthouse, where Mom and Dad kept getting quieter and quieter. The Stillwaters would never let someone they cared about slip away under the ice.

"Look! You're skating backward!" called Anne. It was true. Mrs. Stillwater had let go of Nita's hands, and she was carving out long backward glides.

"Oh, I can't do it when I think about it," said Nita, as her feet automatically started forward again. I wonder if Mom can skate, she thought, but there was probably never any ice in Thailand. Mom probably never had this wonderful flying feeling. Nita skated faster and faster, until she thought she might fly up into the air, right off the ice.

"Cocoa," called Mrs. S. Nita scraped to a stop by the log, breathless and almost dizzy. The hot cup warmed her hands. "You girls have to get to bed," Anne's mother went on.

But Nita sipped her cocoa slowly. She wanted to stay out as long as possible. Out here, everything seemed simpler. The black branches of the trees in the moonlight and the icy pond had been the same every winter for ten thousand years, maybe. It made Nita feel better to think that, though she wasn't sure why.

"Do fish get frozen?" asked Anne.

"No," said Nita. She put down her cup and started to unlace her skates. "Dad goes ice fishing sometimes. He says fish slow way down and lie in the water at the bottom of the pond."

"Girls," said Mrs. S. She picked up her skates and the thermos.

"We're coming," they answered, and started up the slope. The house up above them had lights in the windows, and as they walked toward the warm, yellow glow, a blast of sound came from an attic window.

"What's *that*?" Nita slipped on the path, startled.

"Petrova is playing her whale songs." The weird moaning and clicking echoed out over the frozen woods.

"Weird," said Nita.

"You mean unusual—that's what Mom says. We don't call people 'weird,' just 'unusual.' Listen! Now she's playing her very unusual owl recordings. That's why the window is open, so the owls can hear."

Screeches came from the window and Nita shivered. It was a creepy sound.

It was warm in the house and Anne's room had a chair that folded out into a bed for Nita. She put her stuffed cat under the covers and felt safer. When she was in bed, she could see the moon out the window and her skating feeling came back for a minute. She remembered the flying feeling and the world of black trees and ice that had been there, well, *almost* forever.

Mr. Stillwater came to the door. "Hi, Nita," he said. "If you need any help with your math, don't hesitate to ask." His mouth twitched in a little smile, as if he knew Anne complained about his "help."

"Thank you, Mr. Stillwater," said Nita.

"Oh, call me Bill," he said. "Good night, girls." He shut the door.

Nita sank back on her pillows. Bill? I don't think I could call him that out loud, she thought. Screeches and moans sounded very faintly from the attic. Nita eyed the moon and wondered if her Mom was looking out the window of wherever she was, watching the moon, too.

"Good night, Mom," she whispered.

Five

THE NEXT DAY after school Nita headed out of town, down by the beach. She didn't even look at her house; she was going to Amy Bradley's to talk about the play.

And she was going to stay overnight at Anne's again. Dad said he was staying at the Coast Guard base because the next day he might have to go out on one of the boats. Why does he have to leave when Mom's in the hospital? thought Nita. Even though he always goes to sea, now I do *not* want him to. Not, not, not.

Even school wasn't as safe as usual, because Mrs. Sommers kept asking her about that report. She still didn't know what to write about.

Nita kicked a couple of stones along the edge of the beach, and kept her head down so she wouldn't see the lighthouse. Icy little waves lapped the shore. She was supposed to meet Anne at Amy's house to talk about the play. Anne had been to her piano lesson, and Nita had stayed after school to help Mrs. Sommers clean the guinea pig cage.

And then, all of a sudden, Nita saw it again. Just what she had seen yesterday on the way to school. The white patch of snow flew up in the air again, and this time it didn't vanish. It wasn't snow, it really was a bird, just as she had thought.

Nita caught her breath. It was there. A huge white bird, an . . . *owl*, staring back at her from a low sand dune. The round, unblinking yellow eyes bored into her brain, until Nita squeezed her own eyes shut for just a second. Even then, yellow spots danced on the insides of her eyelids. She stared again, trying to get used to the amazing sight.

Her heart thumped. Would the owl hurt her? It seemed so beautiful, so calm and unafraid, but she could see its huge curved talons clutching the dune grass. Wind ruffled the snowy feathers. The owl didn't seem cold; it seemed completely at home in this icy setting. Nita wished she could feel at home like that, comfortable on an icy sand dune, not needing anything.

Far away, she heard the sound of a truck. The owl's head swiveled, and as the truck came closer, the big bird spread its wide white wings. Nita gasped. With a flap of its wings and a shake of suddenly appearing feathery legs, the owl was carried down the beach by the wind, soared low over the edge of the water, and vanished around the rocky point.

That owl was as big as a . . . as a . . . fire hydrant, she thought as she passed one at the edge of the road. I'll tell Petrova! She'll be so excited! Didn't Anne say Petrova had been going all the way to the airport to band owls, and now here was one right here in town!

She turned into the Bradleys' driveway. The world looked different. The wintry sky was owl-colored, and the bright-brass knocker on Amy's front door gleamed like the owl's yellow eyes. Then Nita banged on the door and the spell was broken.

Amy's house was full of dogs and little boys. Anne was already there, and Nita was caught in a whirl-wind of action. There was no way to tell anyone about the owl.

Finally, the girls shut themselves in Amy's room for a play conference. Her room was crowded with pro-jects—knitting, drawing, and play costumes. On the wall was a blown-up photograph of a green iguana, which at that size looked like a dragon.

"Guess what?" asked Nita.

"You want to be in the play," said Amy.

"Yes, but guess what I saw?"

Amy finally gave Nita her full attention. Her big brown eyes looked out from her wild hair and focused on Nita. "What did you see?"

"A huge white owl! On the beach."

"A snowy owl?" asked Anne.

"Is that what they're called? I can't wait to tell Petrova."

Amy reached for her book of *Snow White.* "Wait a second," she said. "I think . . . yeah, listen. I thought I remembered there's an owl in this story! The story goes: 'And the birds of the air came too, and bemoaned Snow White: first of all came an owl. . . .' "

"I wonder . . ." said Nita, but then she didn't speak her chilling thought aloud. I wonder if *my* owl came because of my Mom. Maybe it came to bemoan *her,* to cry for her, because she was lying so still and not talking, as if Mom were Snow White in her glass coffin. Maybe it came to *get* her. Maybe it means she's going to die.

Nita felt tears prickle her eyelids. "Where's the bathroom?" she muttered. Amy pointed down the hall, and

Nita held her breath until she was safely behind the closed bathroom door.

She stared at herself in the mirror. Her brown face was smooth, her eyes dark. Her bangs parted a little in the middle, as if the wind had blown them apart. She was sad, confused, and scared, and it didn't even show on her face, like it would on, say, Amy's face, with her flushed pink cheeks and wild hair.

Mom was the same way. You could only tell she was upset when she got even quieter than usual. Were people from Thailand always like that? But even if they are always like that, I am only half Thai, thought Nita. I hardly even remember Thailand. Furiously, she messed up half her hair and stuck out her tongue at the mirror, but her silky hair slid back into place, and, after a few seconds, she slid her tongue in, too. She felt silly. Silly, but at least she didn't feel like crying anymore.

And maybe the owl was good. It would bemoan Mom and then she'd get better! Nita remembered the great feeling she had when she saw that huge, snowy bird. As if she were special to have it come near her and look at her with those yellow eyes.

"Nita!" Anne called to her from outside the bathroom door. "Come on, we've got to talk about the parts."

Nita opened the bathroom door. She felt much better, and it was the thought of the wild, free bird that had done it.

"I absolutely want to be a dwarf," said Anne. "I mean, if you pick me. I love to dance and sing."

"What about you, Nita?" asked Amy. She wrote on her clipboard.

"Well," said Nita, "I don't want to be a dwarf." Then she surprised herself. "I want to be—Snow White!"

The words came out as if some new person were speaking them.

Anne bounced up on the bed in surprise. "You *do*?" she said.

"Yes," she said, a bit more firmly, still wondering why. Nothing had happened that was different except the owl. The owl. It had something to do with the owl, and something to do with Mom, and a new feeling that was growing inside her.

Amy gave Nita a considering look. "You'd be a good Snow White," said Amy. "I'll put you down on my list." Then she went back to writing on her clipboard.

"Amy!" came a voice from downstairs. "I need your help, and Anne's mom is here for her and Nita."

The girls thundered down the stairs. There was a flurry of dogs, boys, and good-byes.

Then Anne and Nita were outside for a freezing minute until they got in the warm car.

"Guess what, Mom?" said Anne. "Nita's going to try out for Snow White!"

The old Nita slouched way down in her seat, wishing she'd never said she would do anything so scary.

Six

AT THE STILLWATERS', they found Petrova in the kitchen, bent over her homework. "Want some popcorn?" she said, in a friendly enough way so that Nita didn't feel too nervous to talk to her. The warm smell filled the kitchen and Nita slid onto the bench across from Anne's fourteen-year-old sister.

"I saw a snowy owl," said Nita.

Petrova gave her full attention. "You're sure?"

"A huge white one. Well, it had some brown flecks, and it sat on a sand dune and watched me. Not afraid at all. It was about this big." Nita measured at least two feet above the table. "With yellow eyes! They stared right at me."

"A snowy," said Petrova. "That's so great! That's the kind I've been banding, but I've never seen one here in the Landing."

"I thought owls only came out at night," said Anne.

"Not snowies. They hunt in the day," answered Petrova.

"What do they hunt?" asked Nita, reaching for some popcorn. She remembered the way the owl's head swiveled when it heard the truck. She was sure they were good hunters.

"Oh, little birds. Or animals. They could even eat a Canada goose."

"I wish they would," said Anne. "Those geese make such a mess on the soccer field. Did you know there's an owl in our play? Right there in *Snow White*?"

Nita thought about what Petrova had said. It was unusual for a snowy owl to come here to the Landing. "So why did the owl come just when we were going to have our play?" she asked.

"Like a fairy tale coming to life," said Anne.

"The owl didn't come because of your dumb play," said Petrova sarcastically. "You're having a play. The owl is on the beach. It's called a coincidence." Nita could hear the word "idiot" floating at the end of the last sentence.

"It's not a dumb play," Anne said angrily. "It's an old famous story that a lot of people have liked, even Russians like you!" She turned and stomped up a couple of stairs. "Come on, Nita. Don't talk to her. She tries to spoil everything."

Petrova shrugged her shoulders and looked back at her homework. Nita crept up the stairs after Anne, but Petrova had made her feel better by not believing the owl was any kind of spirit, good or bad. When they reached the safety of Anne's room, Nita said, "You and Petrova sure are different."

Anne's mood changed. She laughed. "Mom says I'm like Dad's mother, who's my Granny, who sends me fairy-tale books. Mom says Petrova is like our other Grandma, who was a scientist in Russia! We call her *Babushka*—that's Russian for grandmother."

"When I was little," said Nita shyly, "I called my Mom . . . *Ma-jah*." The word felt strange on her tongue. "That's how you say Mom in Thai." It was the first time in a long, long time Nita had said even one word in Thai. And that word, just one word, filled her mind with warm air, sunlight through palm trees, and a little lizard sitting on a stone. It was a different world than outside Anne's bedroom window in Maushope's Landing.

For a minute, Nita was very small. She sat by the stone and looked at the lizard. "What is it, Ma-jah?" she asked.

"A lizard," said Ma-jah, and she laughed at the sight of Nita's amazement. "Jing-jok," she said in Thai. Her laugh fell on Nita like the sun through the trees, making little dancing spots of light in her world.

Back on her chair-bed in Anne's room, Nita felt amazed all over again that a word could call up a world. One word had carried her back to the mango farm in Thailand that belonged to her mother's family. It *was* amazing. And even more amazing, and sad, was that Nita had almost forgotten her mother's laugh. Ma-jah hadn't laughed for such a long time now.

The bright green and gold memory faded, and Nita looked out at the winter sky of Maushope's Landing. She pressed her pillow to her chest. She wanted to go home, but there was no home if Ma-jah wasn't there.

Suddenly she wondered if that's how Ma-jah felt about the mango farm. That had been her home. And when she came back to the Landing after her visit, Dad said she was homesick. Nita had never wondered before if Mom missed Thailand. It had always been her and Mom and Dad, the three of them. Thailand was long ago and far away. But did Mom think Thailand was her real home?

Nita rolled over. I don't know, she thought. I just want her to come home! *I'm* homesick. The picture in her mind was of the lighthouse, but now there were palm trees planted out front in the snow.

Anne had picked up her orange fairy-tale book while Nita was daydreaming. She had a set of these books in lots of colors including pink, green, purple, and blue.

"Anne," said Nita, "have you ever had a mango?"

"No," said Anne, looking up from her book. "What is a mango? It sounds like a dance."

Nita laughed. "It's a fruit. A fruit from Thailand—orange inside like the outside of that book."

"*Dee*-licious," said Anne. She pretended to bite off the corner of her book. "Tell me more about this wonderful country."

"I wish I knew more," said Nita sadly.

Seven

DAD CAME and picked Nita up early the
next morning, before school. "We've got to
both get packed, Nita," he said, as they drove through
the Landing. "I've got to go out on one of the boats,
but just for one night, at the very most two." He
looked officially busy, in his blue Coast Guard clothes,
and worried.

"I wish you didn't have to go, Dad," said Nita. "What
about Mom?" She was glad to see that no palm trees had
sprung up in the snow by the lighthouse, though a
string of colored holiday lights encircled the tower.

"I know, I know, but I *have* to go." He unlocked
the door to their house and went off into the kitchen.

His voice said, indistinctly, ". . . testing equipment . . . broken . . ."

Nita wasn't really listening until she heard him say, "I saw Mom this morning . . . you can visit. . . . Mrs. S. will . . ." The house was not very warm, and Dad's footsteps seemed to echo on the wooden floor.

She followed him into the kitchen. Dad was polishing his shoes. He had work shoes and dress shoes and he kept them all perfectly polished. The shoes were neat and thin, like their owner. Nita stuck her foot into the row of shoes. Her dirty sneaker didn't look very Coast Guard–like. Dad pretended to dab some black polish on her sneaker, and she snatched her foot away.

"I'll need some new shoes if I get picked to be Snow White," she said. "Do you think Mom will come to the play? If I'm in it?"

He didn't answer right away. "I think she'd really *like* to come to your play," he said, finally. Dad looked unhappy. The lines in his face were deep and long. He went over to the window and sprayed a few of Mom's orchid plants. They didn't look so great. A few leaves were turning brown and they looked dusty.

Maybe I won't even try out, thought Nita. She felt cold, as if a little piece of winter ice had gotten stuck in her chest. Here she was at home, and it didn't even feel like home.

"Come on, kiddo," said Dad. He sighed as though he were just too tired for discussion. Then he zipped his shoes into his duffel and held the door for Nita. She picked up her duffel bag. On the way to the car, she scooped some birdseed onto the feeder. The birds had not a single seed left. It was Mom who usually fed them.

The wind was strong and the blue water was edged with whitecaps. Nita looked hard at every dune as they drove along the beach. No yellow eyes looked back.

"I saw a snowy owl here yesterday," said Nita.

"Great!" said Dad, but he didn't sound very enthusiastic. He looked over the beach, out across the water. "And Nita . . ." he said.

"I know. I'll be helpful and do my homework and say please and thank you."

"Try not to worry too much about Mom. She has a good doctor, and Mrs. Stillwater will take you to the hospital to see her tonight."

"She *will?*"

Why doesn't anyone ask me if I want to go see her? she wondered. They have it all planned. They have me all packed up and labeled, like my duffel.

"Let's drop off your duffel at the Stillwaters'. Then you've got time to go to the dock before school."

Nobody asks me anything, thought Nita. They just assume I'll do what they plan.

Dad fiddled with the radio on the way to the Stillwaters' and waited while Nita put her duffel in the house. Then they drove down to the Coast Guard base, the radio playing piano music and Nita picking at a hole in her shoe. "I wish you wouldn't go," she said.

Dad parked the car and hurried toward the gate. Nita followed more slowly. See? He just assumes I'll follow him, like a dog or something.

The dock looked like a postcard, with the white cutter, the flags, and the Coast Guard people all dressed in blue. Dad looked more and more cheerful the closer he got to that stupid boat.

"Hey, Nita."

"Hi, kid." Two officers greeted Nita.

Dad gave her another of his one-arm hugs, but Nita couldn't look at him or smile. He ran up the gangplank and jumped down onto the deck.

The whistle blasted and the shore crew loosed the lines. Dad waved to her from the deck, and the icy blue water made a widening space between them, just like in the movies. Nita's eyes prickled and her arm shot up. Then she put her arm down. See, I'm playing my part in this movie, she thought. Acting. I *won't* wave to him; he's being a jerk.

[47]

She turned away and almost missed seeing the captain of the cutter throw something in a high arc toward the dock. A little dog leaped into the air and caught a dog biscuit! The crowd cheered, the shore crew laughed, and Dad's face became a blur under his blue hat. Soon all the dark blue dots on the deck looked the same. The cutter passed the marker buoys and headed out of the harbor into the sound.

Nita reached down and patted the captain's little dog, who had come over and drooped against her leg. *I know how he feels,* she thought. Is it better to be a person? At least the dog got a biscuit.

A big, smiling man with gold on his hat hurried toward Nita. "Hi there," he said. "Everything okay?"

Nita glared at him. She edged toward the gate with the dog at her heels.

"Because if you need . . . I mean, well, have a good day at school!" said the officer. His face seemed to get redder, but it had been red to begin with. Nita remembered him now. Captain Pudge! Only she was sure that was not his real name. He used to go fishing with Dad. His friendly smile wavered as he saw Nita's glare.

"I can't take this dog, though," said Nita. She was trying to be nice. It wasn't his fault that Dad was a jerk.

"Oh, I'll keep him. I always keep him when Dick Turner goes out. Come on, fella. Snack time!" The little dog trotted back inside the gate. Nita headed toward school, feeling hungry.

Now I'm an orphan, she thought, because my parents are both gone. Maybe it will start to snow. There's even a hole in my shoe—it's not a very big one, but it might get bigger. An orphan, all alone in the world.

She stopped at the drugstore and bought yellow Banana Peels chewing gum. Orphans don't usually have any money, she thought, but maybe I earned it selling matches on snowy streets, like in that story Anne is reading.

It was not going to snow on such a sunny day, but it was still freezing cold. Maushope's Landing looked polished by the wind. The trees had not one loose leaf or twig. Stiff gray branches waved against the blue sky and all the buildings looked white in the morning sunlight.

Clang! Clang! Now the old school bell tolled in the belfry. Some lucky person, probably Henry, was pulling on the bell rope. People were supposed to take turns, but he seemed to get more than his share.

Nita was caught in the playground swirl, but she moved through it like a fish through the coral and sharks of a dangerous sea. She found Anne down by the back fence.

"Oh, hi, Nita, thank goodness you got here," said

Anne. She looked as if she hadn't seen Nita for days, though they'd had breakfast together about two hours ago, before Dad had picked Nita up. The ice chip in Nita's chest melted a little bit more. "Remember, Amy is coming here for the tryouts."

"She's not coming until last period," said Brenda. "And anyway, Nita doesn't care about the tryouts," said Brenda. "*I've* been taking acting lessons." She bounced on her toes and tossed her hair. "*I* was in *The Wizard of Oz* at the Maushop Playhouse."

"You were a Munchkin," said Max. "You were a doughnut hole, munch, munch, munch."

"That *is* what they call them at the doughnut shop," said Henry's buddy Pete, imitating the way Brenda talked. He tossed his head, mimicking Brenda with her red ponytail.

"I *wasn't* a doughnut hole," said Brenda, outraged.

Nita saw Henry grin when he saw that Brenda was mad. Then he noticed Nita and made his troll face. His hands curved into claws and he took two giant steps slo-o-wly toward her.

Don't run, Nita said to herself, but her heart beat faster as his face got closer and closer and the claws were—*Clang! Clang!* Only the second bell saved her.

Up in the classroom, the morning crashed and swirled around Nita. She liked the old classroom with the view of masts and seagulls out the window, the class guinea pig Juliet with her gold earring, and the poster that said GIVE THEM BOOKS, GIVE THEM WINGS over a picture of a flying book. But she did *not* like Henry. She couldn't help it—he scared her because she could never tell what he would do next. She remembered those claws right next to her face and shivered. And those tryouts . . . and her report!

She still couldn't think of a subject for her report. Nita opened her binder to a blank sheet of paper. She cleared everything else off her desk. She held up her *Mayflower* pen and made the tiny boat sail back and forth in the capsule of fluid. When it sailed toward the ink end of the pen, the boat sailed forward and arrived at Plymouth Rock, but when it sailed toward the blunt end and headed back toward England, the *Mayflower* went backward all the way. Nita wondered what mayflowers were like, she wondered if this writing period would ever be over, she imagined Brenda as a dancing doughnut hole, she wondered what Mom was doing right this minute. (Mom, in the hospital! Were they doing something horrible to her? Operating on her brain?)

Finally, it was lunchtime. The afternoon was no better. Nita daydreamed until Amy stuck her wild head of hair around the door and smiled at Mrs. Sommers.

"All right, play people," said Mrs. Sommers, "if you're trying out, go quietly—*quietly*, Henry—down to the kindergarten room."

Amy and her friend David were very organized. David took kids who wanted to be in the technical crew, and Amy got everyone who wanted to act. Each person had to sing, walk, and see if they could talk loud enough so Amy could hear them in the back of the room. This cut out a lot of people. Brenda sang the Munchkin song "Lollipop Land," while Henry and Pete stuck their fingers down their throats and made gagging noises.

"If you guys do that anymore, you're out of here," said Amy.

Why did they even want to be in a play, anyway? Nita couldn't understand it. They refused to sing. Well, so did Nita, and Anne looked worried.

"Snow White doesn't sing," Nita told her, and she spoke up loudly so Amy could hear her. "Mirror, mirror, on the wall, who is the fairest one of all?" It was funny how she didn't mind speaking up as long as it wasn't her own thoughts and words she had to say.

Then Amy stuck her pencil into her wild hair, and said, "Okay, now here is the way I think the parts should go."

"But we haven't tried out!" said Brenda. "That's not

the way it was at the Maushop Playhouse, when we had scripts and makeup."

"Well, this is a different kind of play," said Amy. "This is . . . we all know the story, right? So we improvise."

Brenda folded her arms and glowered.

"Right," said Amy. "Now, I pick you for the Wicked Queen, Brenda."

Everyone laughed.

"Noooooo," wailed Brenda. "I don't wanna be the Wicked Queen. I wanna try out for Snow White."

"Brenda, you'll be great," said Amy. "I can just see you biting into Snow White's juicy heart."

"Or your little feet, dancing in the red-hot shoes," said Anne.

"I'm good at dancing," said Brenda. She tossed her ponytail. "So who's going to be Snow White? There's no one who's used to acting but me."

"Nita is going to be Snow White," said Amy.

There was a short silence. Then Henry burst out, "She can't be Snow White. She's not white! She'll have to be Snow Brown!"

Some people laughed. Amy fluffed up like a cat about to scratch. "Don't be stupid, Henry," she hissed. "This is acting. That's the whole point of acting—you *pretend* to be someone else."

Nita looked at the floor. She could feel eyes on her

skin, eyebeams running over her like X rays. They could see even inside of her and see how different she was from everyone else, inside and out.

"Okay, okay," said Henry. "I was only kidding."

"And I pick you for the prince," said Amy. "But I'll take it back if you don't act like one."

For once, Henry had nothing to say. He staggered around, pointing at himself and smacking his forehead, then shaking his head in amazement.

"I'm so excited you got that part!" Anne whispered to Nita.

"I want to be excited," Nita whispered back. "But now . . . I'm kind of scared, and I *don't* want Henry to be the prince."

"That wasn't very nice, what he said. But look at him. He's a very good actor."

Nita guessed even Anne didn't understand how she felt about Henry.

"And Anne, you'll be the head dwarf. Pete, you'll be the talking mirror," Amy went on. She picked the Huntsman and the King and Queen. All the others were dwarfs. There were a lot of dwarfs because, as Anne said, there's no rule that says there have to be seven.

David came over from the technical crew corner. "Who's going to build Snow White's coffin?" he asked.

He and Amy looked at Anne. "Petrova's the best builder," he said. "Will you ask her if she'll help us?"

"I'll ask her as soon as I get home," said Anne. "Come on, Nita. It's time to go, anyway."

"And one more thing," said Amy. "Get out the story and read it when you get home. Then you'll all know what to do for your part. See you tomorrow!"

"Boy, that Henry," said Anne, as they headed up the hill to the Stillwaters'. "Did he make you feel bad when he said you had to be Snow Brown?"

Nita felt her face get hot. "Well, maybe a little. I do look different. At my other school, someone asked me if I could see out of my eyes very well, because they were so little." There! She had told Anne one of her most embarrassing secrets, one that she had never told anyone before.

Anne looked mad, just like Amy had over the name Snow Brown. "Yeah, well, my Mom and I love the way your eyes squinch up when you laugh."

They did? That meant they talked about her when she wasn't there. Nita's face felt even hotter. The Stillwaters talked about everything.

"Don't worry when Amy's around. She won't take anything from Henry. And she's kind of brown herself."

It was true, thought Nita. So, good. "Whose skin is as white as snow, anyway?" Nita said out loud.

"Not Brenda's, she's spotted," said Anne. They came into the house laughing, thinking of Brenda's freckles. "Spotted like a leopard," said Anne.

They found Petrova, as usual, working on her owl model. "I'm going to hang it from the ceiling," she said. "Down on the floor, I'll put a model mouse."

"Ugh," said Anne. "Swooping down on poor little mice."

"That's their nature. You shouldn't criticize an owl for having an owl nature."

Nita tried to keep them from arguing. "Maybe you can put the mouse on a string, too, so we can jerk it away. Oh, Petrova, David wants to know if you'll help him build Snow White's coffin."

Petrova frowned over her paper and glue. "You guys and your fairy-tale projects," she muttered. "Tell him I might help. If I get my owl done."

Petrova wasn't much like Anne. But then, she was getting old. The older people got, the busier they were and the less they did anything interesting. A few older kids, like Amy and David, are still interesting, thought Nita, but I bet people call them childish.

Nita and Anne went into the kitchen and found some saltines and cheese to eat. They nibbled the food like mice and hid under the table. Even Petrova joined in the spirit of things, swooping around the room making weird screeches and moans until they let her have some cheese and crackers. Maybe there was hope for her after all.

But the fun ended for Nita when she found a note on the counter from Mrs. S. It said: "Nita, please do your homework this afternoon, because I'm going to take you to the hospital to see your Mom tonight."

Nita's orphan feeling washed over her like a wave. Maybe the Stillwaters could adopt me, she thought. I don't want to go to the hospital. She felt like getting back under the table and staying in the corner, as small and still as a mouse.

Eight

I WONDER if anyone laughs here, thought Nita as she walked down the long, green corridor with Mrs. Stillwater. The hospital air was hot and stuffy after the winter night outside. As if in answer to her thoughts, a loud laugh rang out from the nurses' station. That made Nita feel worse. They probably think the people in here who have problems are funny, she thought.

"In here, Nita," said Mrs. S. She stopped at a half-open door. "I'll wait for you down there, in the waiting room." She pointed to the end of the corridor.

Nita grabbed her hand to get her to stay, but Mrs. S. whispered, "Remember what we talked about? I know you're a little scared, but it could really help your Mom to have you visit. I'll be right down there if you need me."

Nita stood, frozen, by the half-open door. That mouselike feeling, as if something were going to swoop down and pounce, paralyzed her. No! I don't want to be the mouse! I want to be the owl. I need *that* feeling back to get me through this door, she thought.

"Mom?" she said, and gave a little tap on the door. It swung open. Her mother was lying down. Slowly, Nita walked over and sat on the chair next to the bed. Her chest felt tight and it was hard to breathe. Talk to me, she pleaded silently with her mother. Silence was back in the room with them, like a glass wall they couldn't break through.

Mom looked at the wall at the end of the bed, not at Nita. Nita jammed her hands in her pockets and stared at the wall, too. She took a deep breath and tried to stay calm. One hand fidgeted with something in her pocket. She pulled it out. It was her *Mayflower* pen.

Nita leaned over and showed the pen to Mom. "Remember when we went to Plymouth Rock?" she asked. There was no answer. Idly, Nita tilted the pen so the boat sailed in toward Plymouth Rock. Then she tilted the pen the other way so the boat sailed out to sea again, backward. Then she sneaked another look at

Mom. Mom's eyes were moving! She watched the little boat. Back and forth Nita tilted the pen. Back and forth went her Mom's eyes, watching the little boat.

"Come back, Ma-jah," Nita said softly. Slowly, Mom turned her head and looked at Nita.

She had sent Mom a message and Mom had understood. You went away, Nita said with her pen, you went away, but you can come back.

"Ma-jah," said Nita, "I'm going to be Snow White in the play." She looked at me! Now Nita knew Mom could hear her. She could tell her about the play and about how she went ice skating at night, and Mom would listen.

But the most important thing, Nita decided, was that she wouldn't try to get Mom to talk. I've got lots to tell, and I won't worry about getting an answer, just yet. *I know it's hard to speak up sometimes.*

She leaned back in her chair and smiled at her mother. At Ma-jah. Suddenly, she sat up again. I wonder if that's why she looked at me! Because I called her Ma-jah? Because I spoke to her in Thai? Nita sank back in the chair again, and now Silence seemed more like a friend, leaving space for a few words of Thai to make their music in Nita's memory. *Ma-jah. Jing-jok. Sawadee.* Hello. Good morning. Good night.

Nine

BACK IN HER bed in Anne's room, Nita dreamed of a ship going out and coming back. She dreamed of Dad going out in his Coast Guard cutter, but the ship that returned was the *Mayflower*, manned by dwarfs. A yellow-eyed owl hovered on the ship's bow as a figurehead, wings spread and talons extended. No wonder the ship arrived safely home—any sea monster would be afraid of that fierce-looking owl.

Then it was morning. Nita looked up at the gray sky and gray branches of a winter morning in Maushope's Landing, and then over to Anne's empty bed. The smell of bacon drifted up the stairs. Quickly, Nita got out of bed and started dressing.

"You look just like Snow White," said Anne, when she came back from the shower. "Red as blood, white as milk, and black as ebony. I read the story last night while you were out."

Nita looked at her black jeans, white turtleneck, and red sweatshirt. She hadn't done it on purpose, but it was as if some part of her remembered that today was the first rehearsal. "Now I'm scared," she said as they went down the stairs. "I wish I'd never said I'd be in the play."

"You'll be good," said Petrova. Nita hadn't seen her around the kitchen door, or she might not have said that about being scared. Petrova was probably never scared.

"And Brenda is so witchy, she'll be great," Anne added.

I wonder why Petrova thinks I'll be good, thought Nita. Because I look like I'm lost in the woods? Or because I'm so stupid I'd eat a poisoned apple? That was one thing that bothered her about Snow White. Nita thought about it as she ate her bacon sandwich. Maybe Snow White had never learned to speak up and say, "*No!*"

Petrova and her father talked about banding snowy owls at the airport.

"Are you going to band the one out at the beach by our house?" asked Nita.

"I can hardly believe there's one still out there," said Bill. He wiped his mustache carefully after he drank some coffee. He looked like a sleek walrus this morning, with his hair still wet from the shower. "Maybe that snowy was on her way somewhere."

"Let's go down this afternoon," said Petrova. "We'll look. I went yesterday, but I didn't see her."

"We have a rehearsal today," said Nita. "We could go tomorrow. It's Saturday."

"How's your science paper going, Anne?" asked Bill, the keeper of the family homework.

"Okay. But I have to explain some things, like those balancing stones and stuff. I keep forgetting what you told me about glacial more-whatever-they-are."

"Lots of rock was left in strange places by the glacier," said Bill. He curved his arm across the breakfast table. Slowly, his arm moved over the table, and the coffee mugs, the sugar bowl, and the spoons all crowded together in the crook of his arm as he pushed. "I am a river of ice, sweeping down from the North," he intoned. Then he sat up and took his arm away. "And then it melted," he went on in a more normal tone of voice, "leaving a glacial moraine."

"So it left everything all jumbled up?" Petrova frowned. "A glacial pile of junk?"

"Wait, wait," said Anne. "Let me get that down. 'Glacial pile of junk,' that's a nice thing to say about poor old Cape Cod."

"I thought you were supposed to be looking things up in the library," said Bill, "not just picking your poor old father's brains. What's your report on, Nita?"

"Uh, I'm not sure yet," stammered Nita.

Bill gave her a questioning look. "Better get busy, hadn't you?" he said.

Oh, I hope he's not going to start keeping track of *my* homework, too, thought Nita.

"Let's go," said Anne. "We'll be late to school." When they were out in the hall, Anne laughed. "You had a narrow escape there!"

Nita didn't laugh.

The cold wrapped its freezing gray fingers around the two girls as they stepped out the door. Nita zipped up her collar when an icy draft went down her neck. She clamped her fur earmuffs over her ears. Anne pulled a red ski hat down low over her forehead. They hurried down School Street, and Anne told Nita the Snow White story all the way to school, so she'd be ready for the rehearsal that afternoon.

"In the middle of winter, a beautiful queen sat sewing by the window," Anne began.

The old school sat patiently waiting to be filled, as it had sat on winter mornings for one hundred years. Nita had seen the pictures in the front hall of the school, class photographs that showed old-fashioned boys in caps and high leather shoes and girls with hair ribbons and dresses. Horses and wagons stood in the dirt road outside. Now Henry's mother zoomed up in the yellow school bus and red lights flashed as she unloaded. The old photos faded behind today's bright colors.

Brenda hopped out of the bus, rushed up to Nita and Anne, and pulled off her gloves. One! Two!

"There!" she said proudly. Her fingernails were long and red. "Stick-ons!" She swiveled her wrists high in the air, like a Spanish dancer playing her castanets.

All morning, Nita couldn't think about anything but the first rehearsal. Time raced past quickly and also crept by very slowly. Fast, when she thought about getting up and acting; slow, when she tried to do any of her schoolwork.

Finally, it was lunchtime. The fifth and sixth grades ate in the classroom in the winter, when it was too cold to sit outside. Nita got out her turkey sandwich, with Russian dressing on black bread. Stillwater lunches were different than Dad's.

Brenda sat on the art table next to Pete's desk. She hissed into his ear, "Mirror, mirror, tell me true: do you love my eyes so blue?"

"You're ugly," said Pete.

"That's not what the mirror says!"

"So, I don't know my part."

Brenda tried again, "Mirror, mirror on the wall: who is the loveliest one of all?"

Henry leaned over from the other side of Pete and said:

"Snow Brown and you,
Are the ugly two."

He and Pete got out of their seats and stomped off, laughing and waving their lunch bags. Everyone looked from Brenda to Nita.

"They're really dumb," said one of the dwarfs from where the group of them sat eating their lunches in the science corner. They had started to do things in a group since being cast in the play.

Nita looked at her sandwich, but she felt she couldn't swallow another bite. It didn't help that they were mean to Brenda, too.

After lunch, there she sat with her *Mayflower* pen again, but this time Mrs. Sommers noticed the blank piece of paper.

"You know, Nita, I had an idea for you. You seem to be awfully stuck."

Nita looked up.

"How about doing your report on Thailand?" said Mrs. Sommers. "Maybe your mother can help you."

"My mother is in the hospital," whispered Nita.

"I know," said Mrs. Sommers, "but even so, she really might like to help you with your report. I'm sorry she's in the hospital, Nita. You must miss her."

Nita couldn't answer because she was afraid she would cry. Her throat felt swollen shut. What if this happens when I'm in the play?

I'm going to have to get up there in front of an audience. In a dress, she suddenly realized in horror. Nita bent her head over her paper and started to draw. Anything was better than thinking about the play. Orchids were what came out of the end of her pen—orchids, not mayflowers at all. Nita drew the white, cascading *Coelogyne nitia*, but when she drew the yellow dancing lady orchid that Mom kept on the kitchen counter, the little flower mouths seemed to say, "You'll freeze up. You'll forget your lines. Your face is too brown. Your eyes are too little." The yellow and white flowers laughed and jeered.

Mrs. Sommers passed by and smiled. "Orchids are certainly part of a good Thailand report," she said. "Now try for some words."

After she was gone, Nita crumpled her paper and

threw it on the floor. Then she put her head down on her desk and curved her arm around it. She turned her head sideways on the brown wood and looked at her hand. It was the same color as the desk. Nita wished she could melt right into the desk and be a piece of wood, a piece of furniture, and never have to have any feelings again, ever.

Ten

NITA DIDN'T SEE how she could go to the rehearsal that afternoon. Unfortunately, she hadn't turned into a piece of furniture, and she still felt awful, but the moment never came when she could say no. Amy and David came down from the junior high, and Mrs. Sommers sent the cast down to the empty kindergarten room.

Nita found herself down there along with the others, surrounded by tiny chairs and nature collages. And Amy didn't even start with the play.

"Now we're all going to do some deep breathing exercises," she ordered.

"Except for the tech crew," said David. "We're going

down to the lab to get some plastic for the coffin." He left with his crew.

"Now we're all going to do some deep breathing exercises," said Amy, more impatiently. "Stand apart from each other. Give yourselves plenty of room." Amy shook her curly hair out of her brown eyes and smiled. Just her smile helped even Nita to relax.

"You can't speak loud enough until you know how to breathe," said Amy. "I hate kids' plays when everyone whispers. We're not going to whisper, and we're not going to rush. Breathe in. Let your stomach swell out when you breathe in, Anne. You're holding your breath. Come on, team! Breathe!"

They breathed in. They breathed out. Henry pretended to choke.

"That's pretty good," said Amy. "Now, do you all know the story of Snow White? Did you read it?"

A chorus of "yes," "sort of," and "what?" greeted Amy's words.

She didn't look too worried. "Well, you can say your own words for now, and then later, I'll write it down. See if you have a feeling for your parts. Let's start with the First Queen, sitting and sewing."

Amy made it seem maybe . . . possible. The girl who played the First Queen had a soft voice, but Amy got her to take a few deep breaths and it did help. The words "I wish I had a baby as red as blood, black as ebony, and white as milk," floated out wistfully.

"That's great," said Amy. "That's the end of scene one. Now for the King getting married again after his wife dies."

Brenda bounced up. "I'll wear high heels," she said. She took hold of the King's arm possessively.

He pulled away, but Amy said, "Good, good. You can pull away, but then give in. Come on, look regal."

They got married and marched regally off. "Music, we need music," said Brenda.

"Some of the dwarfs could play recorders," said Nita.

"Great," said Amy. "Now, Mirror! Queen! Come on, here's your big scene."

Brenda flashed her red fingernails and preened in front of the Mirror, which, at the moment, was Pete and a big piece of cardboard. The Mirror laughed at her.

"No laughing!" said Brenda. She stamped her foot.

"Pete, do the regular Mirror stuff first," said Amy. "*Then* laugh at her, that'll be terrific."

"Mirror, mirror, on the wall," chanted Brenda.

This time the Mirror was really admiring. It turned this way and that way, saying, "I think your right profile is even more beautiful than the left."

Nita was amazed. Pete had acted so dumb about being the Mirror that she couldn't see how he had ever been chosen. But now she could see, especially when they got to the second Mirror scene. Pete's voice changed to a sneer, as he told the Queen:

"Beautiful though you are,
Snow White is more beautiful by far!"

He laughed. The Queen seemed to swell up with anger.

"Okay, curtain! Now, Nita. You and the Huntsman."

Nita's heart gave a leap, like a fish jumping out of the water. But her leap only propelled her a couple of steps into the room. She felt like an idiot. She didn't know her part. Everyone would laugh.

The Huntsman took her hand. She tried to pull it away. "You must come with me," said the Huntsman sorrowfully. He held her hand tighter, and Nita followed him.

As they walked across the kindergarten room, Nita saw the bare trees outside the window. What if it was *winter* when Snow White went out in the woods? She shivered. The Huntsman pulled out his sword.

"Listen, I don't want to do this," said the Huntsman.

"What are you going to do?" asked Snow White.

"I'm supposed to kill you and bring your heart to the Queen."

Nita ran behind a tree. "You will never catch me, never, never," she cried out. She felt like a terrified rabbit in the snow. She felt like . . . like her mother must have felt when her family hid from the soldiers in Thailand! Nita froze. The play went on, and gradually Nita became aware of the room that was actually around her. The Huntsman had killed a wild boar. He would give its heart to the Queen so the Queen would believe Snow White was dead.

Nita's snowy tree turned back into a desk as she heard the voices around her. Mrs. Sommers and Miss Pink, the third- and fourth-grade teacher, stood in the doorway. How long had they been watching?

Nita crouched where she was, and the desk turned into the snowy tree again. She watched the Huntsman start back to the castle through the snow. Lightly, she stepped out into the tracks of the Huntsman. But she couldn't follow him. She would be killed if she went back to the castle. Where could she go? She looked all around her and up in the sky. She could see nothing but snow and bare branches. Then she looked at the ground, and there at her feet was a glossy, black feather lying in the snow. She bent down and looked. It must mean something. "I'll go this way," she said. "The way the feather points." Then she picked up the feather and set off through the trees.

The sound of clapping brought Nita out of her dream. Miss Pink and Mrs. Sommers were applauding!

"That's a *great* way for Snow White to find the dwarfs' house, to have a feather point the way," said Amy. "Remember how the story says 'then came the raven?'" Her curls stood on end because she ran her hands through them in her excitement. "This was a good rehearsal. Now, Monday we'll do act two. Everyone practice breathing!"

Nita was still holding the feather. How had this feather gotten into the kindergarten room? It was a beautiful feather, dark and shiny.

"Give me that, Nita, I'll put it with the props," said Amy. She ran her fingers through her hair one more time and grinned at Nita. "So long!"

As Nita put on her jacket out in the hall, she overheard Miss Pink saying to Mrs. Sommers, ". . . had no idea she could act like that!"

". . . shy . . . surprises!" said Mrs. Sommers. Nita could only make out a few words of the conversation.

They're talking about *me*, she realized as she was swept outside in a crowd of kids who were rushing for the late bus. They really think I'm good! She didn't have much time to enjoy this thought before Henry came charging over.

"That black feather came from a vulture, I bet," he

said to Anne. Then he turned and stared at Nita, who was putting on her earmuffs.

"There's a vulture out there, flying around Maushope's Landing! I bet it's gonna eat you!" said Henry loudly, pointing at Nita's bunny fur earmuffs. "Vultures love rabbits!" Then the bus zoomed up. Henry stumbled on, and his mother took him away.

"Good riddance," said Anne.

They headed up the hill, and by the time they got home it was dark.

"Let's get pizza tonight, girls, because Bill and I are go-ing to a meeting," said Mrs. S. They were always going to meetings: saving the school, building a new library wing, and organizing beach cleanups.

"Where's the pizza? I'm starved," said Anne, pulling an almost empty bag of cookies out of the cupboard.

Nita was starved, too. She slumped down in a big chair and stared out the window.

"Nita was really good, Mom," said Anne. "When she had to be lost in the woods, she really *looked* lost."

Nita was still surprised at what it felt like to be acting. It was like being in a different place, a differ-ent world. The kindergarten room had seemed like a real forest, even though at the same time she could see all the little tables and chairs. And the fear she felt had been real fear, even though part of her mind still knew the Huntsman was only another fifth-grader.

Now, here in the Stillwaters' kitchen, Nita thought about Mom and her family, running from the soldiers in Thailand—that's why she had really been able to act scared. Maybe Mom needs to learn about acting, she thought, and how to get back and forth between wherever she is now and our world.

Nita let her mind drift out the window, where a few patches of snow stood out in the dark under the pine trees. Her thoughts were a strange combination of snow and rice paddies, with snowflakes falling in the burning sun.

"What kind of pizza do you want?" asked Anne. Nita came back to Earth with a thud.

"I don't care."

"Well, pick *something*. I hate deciding all by myself."

"Banana pizza."

"Is that what they eat in Thailand?" asked Mrs. S. She smiled at Nita.

"Or coconut pizza," said Nita, joking back. She didn't say, like she usually would, that she didn't know what they eat in Thailand. That she had lived here in the United States since she was five years old.

"I want pepperoni," said Petrova. "You can't have coconut pizza! It's a . . . a contradiction, an opposite thing. If you have one, you can't have the other."

But I like *lots* of opposite things, thought Nita. Snow and orchids. Mom and Dad. Day and night. "Pepperoni *and* banana," said Nita. "Can we have a pepperoni and banana pizza? Please?"

They got a half-baked one and did the bananas themselves. Even Petrova said it was not bad.

When the phone rang during dinner, it was about Dad. "He's delayed, Nita," said Bill. "That was Captain Vanderpost. He'll call again tomorrow, but you might be stuck with us till next week. I hope you don't mind."

"It's . . . fine. I mean, it's nice of you to let me stay," said Nita. She took another bite of pizza.

"Oh, we like you," said Bill. "Even if it means we have to have very weird dinners."

"You mean unusual," said Anne. "Thai pizza! I read something about Thailand today in one of my books, why it's called the Land of Smiles." She started to tell a story about two quarreling children, a dog, a cat, some honey, and a lizard.

"Jing-jok," murmured Nita.

"And they ended up destroying the whole village," said Anne, "so that's why Thai people always smile now and never fight. Did you know that story, Nita?"

"No. But they *do* fight, because I remember Mom

telling me about hiding from the soldiers," said Nita. "It was very scary and her family had to hide."

"See, that's real life," said Petrova, "not your silly old 'land of smiles' fairy tale."

The two sisters glared at each other.

"And here are two real live quarreling children," said Mrs. S. "Stop it, you two."

Suddenly, Nita felt left out, even though she didn't want to argue. She took a last bite of pizza. The spicy meat and the soft, warm fruit made a great combination. She would have to make some for Dad and Ma-jah if they were ever together again. But would she ever have her old home back, the way it was before? Or, like the lost village, would it completely disappear?

Eleven

ON SATURDAY morning it was nice and warm in the kitchen, and it was great to know you didn't have to go out. Bill said it went down to twenty degrees again during the night. Nita was on her second helping of French toast when Petrova came in from the garage, bringing a blast of cold air with her.

"I'm working on my trap," she said to Nita.

"Trap?"

"For the owl."

"We don't want to hurt it!" Nita had forgotten they were going down to the beach.

"Well, we have to catch this owl if we want to band

it," said Petrova. "You put a tag on its leg and then when someone else finds it, you can tell where the owls are flying to. One guy banded a nest of babies up in the Arctic and they found one later in Canada and one in Siberia. That's in Russia! It went that far." She showed Nita a strange combination of two large tin cans taped end to end to make a metal tube, and a kind of wire box.

"Now tell her what you put in the trap for bait," said Anne. "And it's your turn to do the dishes, Petrova."

"We put bratty little sisters in the trap," said Petrova. "Come on, Nita." She threw her equipment to the floor with a clatter and put a few plates in the dishwasher.

"I'm not even dressed."

Petrova fixed a beady stare on Nita like a bird of prey, like the owl, except her eyes weren't yellow. "Well, *get* dressed."

Nita found herself walking toward the stairs. No wonder Petrova likes owls, thought Nita. She's so fierce.

Nita put on her ski underwear, her jeans, and her warmest sweater. Downstairs, she wrapped a huge scarf around her neck, put on her earmuffs, and said good-bye to Anne.

The two girls went over the hill, across the main road, down a path, and across the ferry parking lot. Then they went along the road to the beach by the lighthouse. It was such a gray morning that the light-house was flashing, though its beam was pale in the daylight.

Nita was glad to see the light was still working and to see the garland of Christmas lights circling up the white tower. She had been thinking about home as if it had disappeared in just these few days. She wriggled her chilly fingers and looked closely at every dune for the owl. "I don't see it," she said.

Petrova clutched the stiff folded metal netting that made her trap. In a bag she had fishing line and the taped tomato cans. "I've only got one mouse," said Petrova.

"Will the owl kill it?"

"*If* the owl comes, it can't reach the mouse. It only stomps around on the wire trying to get the mouse, maybe catching a foot in one of my snares."

They trudged along the beach. "Can we go into my house for a minute?" asked Nita.

"I guess so." Even Petrova was cold.

But when they got to Nita's house and opened the door with the hidden key, she was sorry they had come. Someone had been watering Mom's orchids. Who? Someone had left tools and boards in the corner. What was going on around here?

Nita picked up the sprayer and misted a couple of the

orchids, but all their little mouths were open, and they spoke to her again, "Lady bug, lady bug, fly away home, your house is different and your family is gone."

Nita remembered the mean things they had said to her when she was trying to start her report. "Shut up or I won't water you," she told the flowers.

Petrova gave her a sarcastic look. Talking to flowers? the look said.

The girls stepped out again into the wind that swirled around the white clapboard house. The tall light brightened and dimmed. Nita went to the sheltered corner by the bedroom window and dumped some birdseed in the feeder.

"That's a neat feeder," said Petrova. She ran her fingers over the curved roof and examined the fitted wooden pieces of the little house. "Is it from Thailand?"

"I think so. We've always had it, wherever we moved."

Petrova picked up her trap and they went back down to the beach. Nita had almost given up hope when around the point came a ray of white that settled on top of a dune with a stretch of white wings.

"It's a different one!" Nita called to Petrova.

"Where? Oh! This is a male! The pure snowy white one!"

The owl Nita had seen before was white with brown flecks in its feathers. This one was big, but not quite *as* big. It was too far away to see any yellow eyes.

Petrova clattered her trap down onto the sand. She fumbled in her bag. But, she was in too much of a hurry. The little box that held her mouse somehow slid open as she sank to her knees.

A tiny brown body scampered over the sand, hesitated, twitched its nose, and dove under a clump of brown beach grass.

"Rats! Triple rats!" shouted Petrova.

"Don't shout," said Nita in a tense voice. "The owl will go away. We'll think of something. We'll . . ."

"Don't be an idiot," said Petrova. "Now we've got no bait. That's it. We might as well go home."

And I have to go to *your* home, thought Nita. The home of someone who calls me an idiot. Great, really great. How could I ever have wanted to be part of her family? She pressed her hands against her earmuffs so she wouldn't hear one more word Petrova said to her. And she was never going to speak to Petrova again. And . . . an idea jolted into Nita's mind.

"Petrova! Do they . . . do owls ever eat rabbits? Maybe we can fool him with my bunny fur earmuffs!" Nita snatched off the white fur circles and held them out, her fury vanishing in the wake of her great idea.

Petrova frowned. Then she laughed. "Hey, I'll try anything! Take a long piece of this line and tie it on."

Nita worked on the fake bait while Petrova set her trap. She had made loops out of nylon fishing line that could snare an owl by the foot. She tied the loops onto the top of the wire trap. Then she put the bunny fur earmuffs inside the wire mesh cage.

And still the owl sat, a white flash on the top of a dune, almost as if he were watching them, waiting for them.

They had to stop watching him to fix the trap, and when they finally had it ready, the owl was nowhere to be seen.

"Never mind," said Petrova. "Maybe he sees *us*. They have fantastic eyesight. Come *on*! Let's hide behind the dune."

They lay on their stomachs behind a dune about fifty feet away, out of the wind. Nita held the end of the line they had tied to the earmuffs, and every once in a while she tugged the line so the earmuffs twitched. She thought hard about the owl, as if she could will him to come.

"Good idea, this trap," said Petrova.

"Come on, owl," Nita murmured. And suddenly, lying there, Nita felt her wonderful "owl feeling." For a day or two, she had completely forgotten how she had been swept away by the soaring calm of the huge white wings.

She took a deep breath the way Amy had taught her.

"Come on, owl," she said again. Funny, Petrova didn't seem to mind her talking to birds. Maybe she could understand this kind of conversation.

He came fast. He dropped down, his talons out in front of him, his feathery legs extended. His white wings were spread wide and he looked like a wild angel who had decided to swoop down into the ordinary world for a visit. Nita held her breath.

The owl gripped the wire mesh with his talons. Nita twitched the line. The powerful feet trampled back and forth, trying to get to the pieces of white fur.

Suddenly, the huge bird pulled away and fell over sideways. Nita jumped up. Oh no! Was he hurt?

"It's okay," said Petrova. "We've got him! Come on!" She ran toward the struggling bird, and Nita followed more cautiously. Those feet looked dangerous.

But in seconds, Petrova had him in a firm grip. One hand held both feet and her other arm was around the wings. The owl was still. Nita came closer, and the fierce yellow eyes stared into hers.

"Is he okay?" she whispered.

"Get the cans," said Petrova. "Oh, he's fine, Nita. Now we've got to band him." She didn't seem to feel the way Nita did at all. To her this was technical, like pictures in a how-to book. To Nita, it was like catching the sun, or an angel in your arms.

"The cans, Nita," said Petrova again.

Nita found the metal tube and helped Petrova ease the owl into the cans head first. Gently they set the tube on its side on the ground. The owl didn't struggle at all. He didn't make a sound. Now all that could be seen of him were his feathery legs and fierce talons.

Quickly, Petrova found a metal tag in her bag and slipped it around his ankle. She squeezed the tag shut with pliers. Nita read the words engraved in the aluminum: Advise Fish & Wildlife, Washington D.C., and a number.

"Wonder where he'll go next," said Petrova. "Do you want to take him out?"

"Oh, *yes*," said Nita. She wasn't afraid of him anymore, and she hated seeing him in the tin can. She couldn't wait to get him out.

"Hold him like I did," cautioned Petrova.

Nita got hold of his feet, and they stood him up, still inside the cans. As the tube slipped off over his head, Nita put her arm around him. He was heavy and very warm and soft. Nita held on. "Good-bye," she whispered, and let go of his wings. Instantly, he spread them, and Nita released his feet with a little down and then up motion. It couldn't have been enough to throw him into the air, but he caught the rhythm and the wind took him. He soared over the dune and was swept down the beach until he was a white dot in the distance that finally dissolved in the winter sky.

"I need my earmuffs," said Nita. "I'm freezing." As she covered her ears with soft fur, she remembered the downy warmth of the owl in her arms before she released him into his real world, the sky.

Nita laughed. She took off and ran down the beach. She held out her arms like a pair of soaring wings and the wind blew her. She soared, laughing, all the way to the end of the sand.

Breathless, she ran back to Petrova. "That was so great," Nita said.

Even Petrova smiled. "We were really lucky," she said. "Lots of times they get away."

I forgot I was never going to speak to her again, thought Nita. Oh, well. I can't be mad at her after she let me hold the owl. They walked back to the Stillwaters' in a friendly silence. The day was so bright with sun on the snow, and the memory of the wonderful bird, that she hardly noticed the long walk back.

Twelve

THE STILLWATERS' woodburning stove made the living room cozy on this chilly afternoon. Anne played the piano. Petrova sat in front of her paper owl model, made of hundreds of tiny cutout pieces. It wasn't flat but rounded, a three-dimensional model.

Nita slid onto the other chair at Petrova's card table and watched Petrova fit A to B and E to F.

"Do you have another pair of scissors?" she asked.

Petrova shoved them over. Nita began to snip at a big scrap of paper. She cut bits of paper off the edges here and there, and the round head and streamlined body of the owl appeared. The feathery legs and huge talons were a little harder. But in a few minutes, Nita trimmed out quite a believable owl.

Anne stopped playing the piano and looked at Nita's creation. "It's a shadow puppet," she said.

"I think . . . I think they have them in Thailand. When I was little I saw a show," said Nita, suddenly re-membering. Like the lizard moment, another picture flashed into Nita's mind. A warm summer night with lanterns hung in the trees and huge black shadows sword fighting on a white screen. Nita had sat on a wooden bench and leaned on someone's knee, but she couldn't quite remember whose knee it was.

Now, in the Stillwaters' living room, Anne aimed the lighted lamp at the wall and Nita held up her cutout. A big black shadow soared around the living room.

"Eek!" said Anne. Even Petrova looked a little sur-prised. "It's a really good owl. Maybe we could use it in the play," Anne went on.

"Ma-jah says in Thailand owls are evil spirits," said Nita. She *hadn't* remembered this until she made the shadow leap across the wall.

"That's ridiculous," said Petrova. Nita bounced the owl shadow on the shadow of Petrova's head and Petrova shrank back in her chair.

"So there!" said Anne.

Petrova glared at them.

Nita wasn't the least bit sleepy that night as she lay on her bed in Anne's room, looking at the moon through the trees. The moonlight was not the friendly, pulsing light of the lighthouse, which was put there by people to help people. The moon was bright but cold. Maybe it didn't care about people. Petrova would say it didn't. Like the owl, thought Nita. Like the owl, which isn't *my* owl, the moon isn't *my* moon.

But it drew her. The moonlight on the snow. The cold, lonely winter outdoors, when everyone else was in their cozy houses. Except I'm not in *my* cozy house. I'd like to be out there with my . . . *the* owls!

Nita felt hotter and hotter. She looked at Anne, who was asleep with the blue fairy-tale book on her chest and the bedside light shining on her eyes. Nita turned out the light and went over to the window. She thought of the stars and the owls. The snowy owl sleeps at night; I wonder where?

She went out into the hall, down the stairs, and put her jacket and Anne's old snow pants over her pajamas. She grabbed her skates. The front door clicked loudly as she opened it, and she froze for a few seconds, but no voices called out. Nita knew you were never supposed to skate without a buddy, but she slipped out the door anyway.

It was not very cold and Nita could see lots of stars. She slid down the slope behind the house. Quickly she laced her skates and picked her way to the edge of the frozen pond. With one long swoop, she glided out into the middle of the ice. She skated backward. She twirled with her arms over her head. She tried a little jump, but it wasn't much like a triple toe loop in the Olympics. She tried another jump, a little higher. *CRACK!*

Was she imagining the long line that stretched like black lightning across the ice? *Crack! Crack!* The ice thundered and trembled.

Nita's feet broke through the thin skin of ice into the freezing water. She threw herself flat on the ice, but she was far from shore.

"Ma-jah!" she croaked. "*Chuiy duiy!* Help!"

Now she couldn't feel her legs. "Ma-jah," she sobbed. She flailed her arms up and down as if they were giant wings. It was working! She thrashed her way forward and after a long minute, she felt her knees buckle and her feet touch the bottom. Sobbing, she struggled to the shore and crawled out on her hands and knees. Her feet were totally numb.

Nita's teeth chattered and her body shook as she sneaked in the Stillwaters' front door and up to Anne's room. She stripped off her wet clothes, yanked on her long johns, and huddled under her quilt.

She was still terrified and shaking, but she whispered over and over, "I saved myself. I didn't drown. I saved myself. I didn't drown."

Thirteen

BEFORE NITA even got out of bed on Sunday morning, she heard an unfamiliar voice in the kitchen. Rumble, rumble, she heard, like the cello, then a higher voice like the flute part, then an even lower rumble like the double bass. The double bass is probably Bill—he has a very low voice. But who is the cello? Nita wondered.

She sat up. Where were her clothes from the night before? She found clean jeans and put them on over her long johns. It was only eight o'clock. What was going on down there so early on Sunday morning?

Halfway down the stairs she stopped.

". . . not doing schoolwork . . . outside skating in the

middle of the night . . . why the hell is her father away at a time like this?"

Nita couldn't move. They were talking about her dad. And what Bill said about Dad was true! But Bill sounded angry at *her*, too. An outer door slammed.

Then she heard the flutelike tones of Mrs. S., who poked her head around the kitchen door and saw Nita on the stairs. "There you are! Come and have some breakfast. You have a visitor." She seemed the same as always and Nita's knees unlocked.

In the kitchen, she saw that Captain Pudge was standing in the middle of the room. He was as big as the refrigerator. Bill is gone, thank goodness, thought Nita. She made herself very small in the corner of the breakfast table and stared down into her orange juice glass. She knew she should say hello, but before she could get up her courage, Captain Pudge spoke. "Hi, there, Nita."

"You're the person Dad goes fishing with," she heard her own voice say, finally.

"I wish he were here now," said the Captain. "Then we might get in some ice fishing."

Suddenly Captain Pudge looked embarrassed and shifted from foot to foot. Maybe he hadn't meant to say anything about ice, thought Nita.

Mrs. S. put a plate of pancakes in front of her and headed for the stairs.

"Well, Nita," Captain Pudge said as he sat down across from her, "I have an idea to do something while your Dad's away. I wonder if you'll think it's a good idea."

He was asking *her* if he had a good idea? Nita put a big bite of pancakes in her mouth.

"About your Mom . . ." He stopped, embarrassed.

Nita thought, I know how it feels when you're trying to tell someone something and you just can't get it out. But what can Captain Pudge do for Ma-jah?

"Those flowers of hers, I've been watering them, and that got me thinking."

Nita was so surprised that she said, "What do you want with *them*?"

"I want to make her a better window. Out at your house. So her orchids will grow better." He shoved a picture across the kitchen table. "It will get lots of sun, and look, lights along the side for when the day is dark, or, like now, winter. And a tray of stones so it doesn't matter if the water spray gets on the floor."

Underneath the picture it said DOUBLE GLASS. It showed a window that was twice as big as the little windows in the house by the lighthouse. "Well?" said the Captain.

This was not the moment to be tongue-tied, a joke Dad used to make about her, only he spelled it *tongue-thai-d*.

"It's great!" said Nita, relieved that this conversation was not about herself at all; it was about Ma-jah. She beamed at the Captain. "Is that why there were tools in our kitchen?"

The Captain smiled back and let out a deep breath. "I got the stuff together but I want to be sure you think she'll like it."

"I'm sure. I'm sure she will."

"So, will you come out to the house with me?"

"Well, okay." Nita felt more doubtful. "But . . . do you know when Dad's coming back?"

Now the Captain looked worried again. "They put in to Boston, but now they've gone back out, and he went with them. You know how stubborn he is. He wants to get that system working right."

"That's not why he went back out. It's because Mom isn't home. I don't think he wants to be home without her."

There! It was out. Captain Pudge looked uncomfortable, but he didn't say anything.

For a minute neither of them spoke. Then Nita asked, "What *is* your real name, anyway?"

He laughed. "Al Vanderpost, but I know what they call me!" His big body shook with laughter. "Now, let's get going, if you've finished those flapjacks."

Nita laughed. "Can Anne come too?"

"Sure."

Nita ran upstairs to find her. She met Mrs. S. at the top of the stairs. Mrs. S. smiled. "Oh, Nita," she said, "I want to tell you not to worry if you heard Bill sounding grouchy. His bark is worse than his bite."

"His bark?"

"He won't bite you. He likes you but he's worried about you."

Nita wasn't sure this was true. "Can Anne come with me to my house?" she asked.

"I'm coming," called Anne from her room. Nita went in to put her shoes on. "I told them I went with you to the pond last night," Anne said softly. "But Nita, I was scared when I saw the hole in the ice."

"You can go, Anne," said Mrs. S., coming in the door. "Nita, Bill is worried for a good reason. That was not smart to be out on the ice last night. Think how we'd feel if anything happened to you." She put Nita's dry clothes on the bed.

"I'm sorry," whispered Nita. Then she put her head down and tied her shoes. When she looked up, Mrs. S. was gone.

As Nita and Anne rode through the quiet morning streets of Maushope's Landing with Captain Pudge Vanderpost, the car splashed through puddles of icy mud. The sun was out. Nita's heart lifted as they drove along the beach and the lighthouse came into sight, and then it fell again at the thought of the empty house. Rise and fall, rise and fall, like the little waves breaking along the beach, thought Nita.

Nita got the key and they went in. The house didn't seem so empty with Captain Pudge inside. He was so big, he made the chairs and tables look little.

"See now, these orchids," he said. "They're all crowded in over here, but they sure are pretty. Look at this one, like moths all over the branch." He picked up the spray bottle and began to mist the greenery. "The new window will go right here, easy as pie. The frame's the same size as the old one, but it bows out, see. You think your parents won't mind? Maybe I'm too used to thinking of all the Coast Guard houses as my own."

"I think they'll love it," said Nita as she poured birdseed into a cup. "I'm going to feed the birds," she said, and started out the door.

The Captain peered out the window. "I see you're using your spirit house for a bird feeder," he said. "What does your Mom think of that?"

"Spirit house?" asked Anne. This was her kind of subject.

Nita put down the birdseed. "We've had that bird feeder for a long time."

"In Thailand, there's always a little house like that next to your house so the good spirits will stay nearby and watch out for you."

"How do you know that?" Nita asked him.

"I was in Thailand, same as your Dad, same Loran station. And . . . well, I don't usually tell people this, but I had a Thai wife, too. Then I . . . lost her. She died in a car accident." For a minute his big face drooped. Then he smiled at the girls. "It was a long time ago. But it's one reason I like knowing your Mom."

Nita went out to feed the birds. This was too much to take in all at once. No one had ever said one word to her about spirit houses and Captain Pudge's wife. Or could she possibly not have been listening?

She examined the bird house. The birds didn't actually go inside but got their seed on the large tray the house was nailed to. Suddenly, Anne was there, peering through the dark door of the spirit house. "I don't see anything," she said doubtfully.

"You don't *see* spirits," said Nita.

"Now you sound like Petrova."

The Captain came outside.

"I have an idea, too," said Nita. "To cheer up my mother. Do you think if I spoke Thai to her, that would help? I mean, I've almost forgotten, but I could try. And maybe then she'd tell me about the spirit house and things." As she spoke she felt more and more doubtful, but the Captain gave her a big grin.

"See, that's a great idea. I was thinking when I watered those plants—those roots. What she needs are roots, and Thailand is where she has her roots. It would be great, Nita, it would be like water and light for her orchids, keeping her past alive, sort of. Tell you what. We'll be a committee. Not a very big committee, with only two people on it, but a committee. The Roots Committee!"

He looked so pleased that Nita couldn't laugh. He held out his hand and Nita shook it. His hand was so big that her hand vanished for a minute. It was like shaking hands with a bear.

"I want to be on the committee, too," said Anne.

"It's a deal," said the Captain, shaking hands with her as well.

As Nita finished feeding the birds, she felt a warmth inside that didn't go away in the cold wind. The Roots Committee. But would it work? Would Ma-jah come home?

Fourteen

MONDAY MORNING came all too soon, with Bill ordering everyone around. "Petrova, take out the trash. Anne, don't forget your piano music. Nita!"

"Yes?"

"After school, report to the base. You have a radio date with your Dad."

"Aye, aye, sir!" she said, the way she sometimes did to Dad. Then she felt bad because Anne's Dad wasn't her Dad. Nowhere near as nice as her Dad. Suddenly she missed her father so much that all the air went out of her chest and she felt deflated, like a limp balloon.

Bill stopped in the hall and looked at her with a

little grin. "Well, don't forget to go to the base." Then in the kitchen, she heard him say to Mrs. S., "She's perking up."

Nita took a double-deep breath. But later, in school, she felt definitely *un*perked. School, home, the Stillwaters, and Thailand. She'd like to put them each in their separate folder and think about them one at a time. But they wouldn't stay separate. And then there was the play.

Nita was still thinking about this when she walked over to the library with the others who had not made much progress on their reports. They took the shortcut on the snowy paths and came out behind the building, breathless and laughing.

Nita sat down at one of the big wooden tables and idly turned the pages of a book on flowers she found there. She turned a few pages and suddenly she slid right into a lush jungle world of orchids. She had a strange feeling of actually being there.

Then she closed her eyes. She saw snow, the icy path to the library, her friends laughing, their pink cheeks, Anne's red hat.

She opened her eyes. Orchids, vines, jungle green. The silent mouths of orchids. Her mother's face seemed to be right there, in the book. Did Ma-jah get stuck in this world? Nita wondered.

"Nita!" said Ms. Keene the librarian. "Is that book helping you? Do you need another?"

"Do you have . . . a book about Thailand?" asked Nita.

"Look in the low 900s," said the librarian, pointing to the nonfiction section.

Nita went off to the back shelves, where Anne was looking at science books. "Anne," Nita whispered, after a short search, "you'll never believe this." She held out the book she had found: *Talking of Thailand.*

"Neat," said Anne. "Are you going to do your report on Thailand?"

"I guess so."

"Look up those houses," said Anne. "You know, that the Captain talked about."

And there it was, on page 50: "spirit houses." Nita sat down on the floor and started to read. It was as if she already knew a lot of things in this book, things she had known once and had forgotten.

Here was the lizard she remembered, here was the story of the two quarreling children. There was even a recipe for the peanut sauce her Mom sometimes made!

"Anne, I even found out how my parents got married. Mom was a 'war bride.' " Nita stuffed her book in her backpack.

"But I still want to know about those spirit houses."

"This book says the houses keep bad spirits away

from your house. But Captain Pudge says the houses are for good spirits. I'll have to ask Ma-jah what she thinks, if . . . she'll talk," said Nita. What if Ma-jah doesn't talk? The warm glow of her excitement began to ebb. Her confused feeling was creeping in like fog as she and Anne came out onto the stone steps of the library. She looked at the sky. It was a dull, low gray with not a—*Splat!* A snowball landed on the front of her jacket.

Up ahead, Henry jumped up and down like a lunatic. He clasped his hands over his head and congratulated himself on his awesome aim.

Nita ran down the steps and molded some snow in her mittened hands. *Paf!* She landed her snowball in the middle of Henry's back as he turned and ran. Suddenly, the day seemed brighter. Another snowball at the ready, Nita ran along the path toward school.

Nita had her book under her arm as she headed for the Coast Guard base after school. A seaman near the gate told her where to wait for Lieutenant Cooper, who was going to take her to the radio room. Nita sat on a chair covered with shiny red plastic and looked at *Talking of Thailand.* On the cover was a picture of a canal boat loaded with food, cooking pans, firewood, and other things for sale. Very different from the boats in Maushope's Landing.

"Hi, Nita!" said Lieutenant Cooper's cheery voice, and *zip!* Nita was back from Thailand, in the Landing, at the door of the radio room on the Coast Guard base.

The radio room was filled with the sound of crackling voices from the ceiling speakers. Computers, radio equipment, and file drawers marked SECRET crowded the small space, but it was made homey by a vacuum cleaner in the corner and a banana on the desk. A mirror with stars and stripes on the frame hung on the wall.

Nita shook hands with the radio operator when Lieutenant Cooper introduced her.

"Sit here and hold this," he said, "and push this button when you want to talk."

"*Sqwaaaak* Coast Guard Cutter *Islandia* 02 *screech* over," said the radio.

The radio operator said into the microphone, "This is Coast Guard Group Maushope's Landing. Over."

"Nita!" Dad's voice boomed out of the speaker. "How's my girl? Over."

"Dad!" said Nita. Then she remembered to push the button on the microphone. "Where are you?"

Silence.

"Remember to say 'over,' " said Lieutenant Cooper.

"Over."

"We're near Boston. But we're having a little trouble with the . . . *whoosh. Crackle.*"

"Bad connection," said the radio operator. "There's a storm up there. Tell him your news. I think he can read us."

"I'm okay," said Nita. Then, in a rush, she went on, "And Captain . . . Vanderpost and me and Anne have a plan called the Roots Committee. I'm going to speak Thai to Mom. Over."

"Speak Thai? What for? Her English is perfect."

"I'll explain it when you get here. When are you coming back?"

There was a long, echoing silence.

"Over."

"Love you, kiddo." Dad's voice wavered close and then far away, as if winds were blowing it around over the Atlantic.

"Love *you*, Dad. Come. Back. Home. Over."

Whooooosh. Crackle. Did the winds waft them a faint "O.K."?

"I think he reads you," said the radio operator.

Lieutenant Cooper gave Nita the thumbs-up sign. "I think you got your message through, loud and clear."

It's as hard as talking to someone on another planet to get your parents to listen to you sometimes, thought Nita. "He sounds a lot farther away than Boston," she muttered. The lieutenant smiled sympathetically.

Nita said good-bye to Lieutenant Cooper and the radioman and plodded back up the hill to the school and her rehearsal.

Fifteen

"PLACES!" called Amy.

"Faces!" called Henry, pulling his eyes sideways so he looked at Nita out of little slits.

Is he making fun of my face again? Nita glared at him.

Pete held the cardboard mirror in front of Henry, who was now making a pig face by pushing up his nose.

> "What an ugly pig I see
> Snow White will never marry thee"

said Pete.

Henry laughed and made an even worse face by

pulling the sides of his mouth up with his thumbs and the corners of his eyes down with his first fingers, meanwhile sticking out his tongue.

Amy stood with her hands on her hips, moving her lips as though she were counting to ten to keep her patience. "This is what I get for practicing in the kindergarten room, I guess," she said. "Let's get started if you're finished with the baby act."

Nita stood outside the wooden window frame. It was set on one of the little tables to suggest the dwarfs' house. The dwarfs hung around their house, getting ready for work.

"Sssst. Nita!" Pete pointed to where she should go.

Nita stepped into the dwarfs' house.

"Oooooh," said the dwarf named Sloppy. "Ooooh, look! A beautiful girl!"

"Where did you come from?" asked Grouchy.

"I came from ... the Palace. They left me in the woods to die," said Snow White, and her voice trembled. The dwarfs clustered around her with extra sweaters and pretend cups of cocoa.

Amy put her first finger and thumb together and flashed an approving sign at Nita.

Then the dwarfs pulled on their hats and marched off to work, singing, "Heigh ho, heigh ho, we think it's going to snow!"

Snow White took her broom and swept the floor. She hummed the dwarfs' song. She glanced out the window. Who was *that*? A bent old woman hobbled down the front path.

The disguised Queen wore gloves to hide her fabulous fingernails. "Come out, my pretty, and see what I have for you," she quavered. She pulled ribbons and laces out of her sack.

And so, as the play went on, Snow White fell for the old crone's suggestions, and first she was laced too tight, then she was poisoned with a poisoned comb. After each visit the dwarfs came home and revived her, warning her not to be so trusting.

But the old crone tricked Snow White a third time. The poison apple looked delicious.

"No," said Snow White, "no, thank you." She remembered how she had been laced up so tight she couldn't breathe. Take nothing from strangers.

"Oh," said the old crone, "you seem so lonely here in the woods where no apple trees grow. Look, I'll take a bite myself." Juice ran down her chin as she crunched into the apple. "The rest is for you."

Snow White couldn't stop herself. She reached her hand through the window. The apple felt cool in her hand and the taste was tangy. But as soon as the bite of apple slid down her throat, she swooned to the floor, as if dead. The floor was hard on her back and her nose itched from chalk dust that drifted down from the blackboard tray.

The Queen ripped off her gloves and danced around outside the dwarfs' house. Then she ran back to the castle to look in her Mirror.

"Mirror, mirror, on the wall
Who is the fairest one of all?"

"You, unfortunately," said the Mirror. It made a face at the Queen.

"Great," said Amy. "Now, we have one last scene for today. Nita, you were terrific. Come on over here."

It took Nita a minute to realize that Amy was talking to her. She still felt like Snow White. She almost felt dead. She moved slowly over to Amy's side and brushed some chalk dust from her arm.

David and Petrova carried in the coffin and helped Nita get inside. "Don't roll onto the sides," said Petrova. "It's not stuck together all that tight."

Nita lay down in the clear plastic coffin and David closed the lid. Nita knew there were air holes, because she could see them, but she felt suffocated all the same. She saw Amy's mouth moving and heard her say something, but she couldn't make out the words. She lay very still and tried to breathe so the audience wouldn't notice, and she imagined an owl outside on a tree branch or perched on the classroom flag holder. Bemoaning her.

Is this how Ma-jah feels? As if there is a wall of plastic between her and the rest of the world? Shut off from the world, she can't hear, can't speak, and can only see people out there through the plastic glass? That's it, exactly. Mom has somehow gotten out of this regular world and now she can't get back in.

The coffin wobbled. Nita pressed her hands against the sides so she wouldn't roll as the dwarfs heaved the coffin onto their shoulders. "Stop!" Nita yelled, but no one seemed to hear her.

"Oh woe, oh woe, it's through the woods we go!" sang the dwarfs, stomping their boots.

Nita slid toward her head and then her feet inside the plastic box. "Put me down!" she yelled. Then she sat up, banging her head against the lid, and bursting out of the coffin. The dwarfs stopped stomping and the coffin lurched.

Nita crashed onto the table on her hands and knees.

"Okay, don't have a heart attack," said Anne.

"Guess that poison apple got unstuck from her throat," offered Henry from the sidelines.

"Rehearsal's over!" called Amy. "You'll get used to it, Nita."

Not ever, thought Nita. I won't get used to it, and I won't let Ma-jah get used to it, either.

Sixteen

"YOU SURE yelled," said Anne, as they trudged up the hill in the dark to the Stillwaters' house. "I never heard you yell before."

"I did yell loud, didn't I?" said Nita, stomping through the slush. "But it was just so awful, feeling stuck in there! I didn't even yell like that when I fell through the ice."

"Maybe you should have," said Anne. "Maybe I'd have heard you and we could have helped."

"I always hate yelling. But in the coffin, it made me feel better."

"I bet! I wouldn't like to get in that coffin!"

The two girls shivered in the dark.

Anne's house looked as cozy as the dwarfs' cottage when the girls got closer and could see through the front windows. A light shone out into the cold street and they could see Mrs. S. in the kitchen window.

They burst into the warm front hall, shedding coats and boots. "I'm starving," called Anne, as usual.

"So come and help me," her mother called back. Then Nita remembered that tonight Mrs. S. was going to take her to the hospital again to see Ma-jah. Nita's strong, bursting-out-of-the-coffin feeling began to slip away. But maybe she's better, Nita told herself. I'll take my owl cutout and tell her about the play. Nita went out on the sun porch to get her shadow puppet, which she had glued to a stick.

"Nita!" called Mrs. S. "Better come now, dear, we're going to eat." She gave Nita a questioning look. "Are you okay? Did you talk to your Dad?"

"I talked to him, and I tried to talk to him about Mom, but I'm not sure he heard me," said Nita. "It's hard talking on the radio." As she began to eat her soup, she wondered what Ma-jah was like when *she* was eleven years old. When Ma-jah was my age, she thought, was she like me? It was hard to imagine a girl in Thailand being the same as herself. A girl who grew up on a mango farm and went to shadow puppet shows and then married a tall, pale person in the Coast Guard at the Loran station in Thailand. That's what acting did—it made you think what it would be like to be someone else.

The drive to the hospital seemed even longer tonight. Nita watched the dark sky flow by the tops of the even darker trees.

After the dark drive, the lights in the hospital were very bright and the air was hot. Mrs. S. wandered off toward the waiting room with a preoccupied look, her mind probably already on the pile of papers in her briefcase.

Nita clutched her owl cutout, took a deep breath, and pushed open the door.

Mom was up! At least, she was sitting in a chair.

"Mo—Ma-jah?" said Nita softly. She walked over and sat on the edge of the bed. Mom still seemed far away. But she looked at Nita and smiled a little smile. Then she reached over and took Nita's hand. Their two hands lay together on the bedspread, and for a few minutes no words were needed.

The changed feeling in the air was as delicate as a gauzy fabric that might tear if a loud voice or a sudden movement cut through it. Nita kept her voice soft and low as she began. "Once upon a time, there was a queen. . . ."

She told the whole story.

Ma-jah even smiled at the dwarfs' song.

Finally, Snow White lay in her coffin.

When the owl cutout flew in and swooped down to-ward Snow White, Ma-jah's breath hissed in. She was not looking at the puppet but at the shadow on the wall.

"Owls are bad luck," she whispered.

"I don't think so. Really! This is the owl that came to bemoan Snow White. It feels *sorry* for her." Nita moved so the shadow was not on the wall. Still, Ma-jah turned her head away.

"No, don't," said Nita urgently. "Listen! And then came the raven, but at last came the dove. And it's a real mystery, too," Nita went on, "because I saw a terrific snowy owl, and Petrova and I even banded it! And I found a black feather on the floor to point the way for Snow White—maybe it was a raven feather. But we haven't seen the dove."

Nita's voice died away. She remembered the dove's sad call that almost made her cry when Anne imitated it. Ma-jah had talked, but now Nita was afraid she would slip back into silence, like a fish that came to the surface and then sank down again, back into the deeps.

Nita couldn't help it, she felt so sad that she heard her own voice whisper, "I wish you would come home."

Ma-jah looked at Nita. She didn't turn away. She didn't close her eyes. Then she said, in the most normal voice, as if she had never had a problem in the world, "The only doves I remember in the Landing live under the railroad bridge in the ferry parking lot. Doves . . . are pigeons."

Nita gave a little snort of laughter. "And no one can park their car in that part of the lot because the birds are so messy. I hope that pigeon is not going to mess up Snow White's nice plastic coffin."

Ma-jah's brown eyes looked into Nita's. Was there a twinkle of laughter in her eyes for just a second?

"I'll get the dove to sit near my enemy, Henry," Nita said. Her smile grew bigger. "My enemy, the Prince."

Then Ma-jah leaned back in her chair and closed her eyes.

"I think she's going to sleep," said Mrs. S. quietly. When had she crept in? Mrs. S. beckoned to Nita, who tiptoed out into the hall, carrying her owl puppet.

"That was really nice. I bet your mom loved it."

"Did you hear her talk? She talked to me!"

"That's wonderful," Mrs. S. said, and squeezed Nita's arm.

"I think she was even trying to cheer *me* up. So, can she come home now?"

"Oh, the doctor will have to decide."

Nita looked back at Ma-jah's door. Ma-jah was still in there, stuck in her glass coffin, but at least now she had talked through the breathing holes.

Mrs. S. and Nita drove through the dark night back to Maushope's Landing.

"Do you think they'll let her come home soon?" Nita asked again. "Do you think she'll come to the play?"

"Well, it would be nice." But Mrs. S. didn't say, "Yes, of course."

As they came into town, Nita could see the flash of the lighthouse. Suddenly she longed for her own room, for Dad polishing his shoes, and the smell of curry coming from the kitchen. Maybe soon she could be back there.

When they got to the Stillwaters' house, Nita rushed past Bill and Petrova, who were working on the owl model at the card table. She hurried up the stairs and flopped down on the end of Anne's bed.

"Guess what? Mom talked!"

"Oh, Nita, that's so nice. What'd she say?" Anne put her finger in the orange fairy-tale book to hold her place.

"She was scared of the owl for a second, but she made a joke about the dove! She said they're like the pigeons under the railroad bridge, the ones that make such a mess."

Anne laughed. "So that's the famous dove."

"I'm going to make the dove sit over Henry in the play."

"Good idea. And then in real life, we'll be like the wicked queen and say, 'Oh, Henry, wouldn't you like to take a nice walk with us, under the railroad bridge?' Anyway, I'm glad you're here. Dad and Petrova are being awful."

"What did they do?"

"Oh, they made me do math for hours. And they said mean things about my rock report because I found out some neat stuff about the native Americans, the first people who lived around here. There are stones that they *carved*, but Dad and Petrova call them ventifacts and say the wind did it. *Plus*, they laughed when Henry called up."

"*Henry* called up? On the phone?"

"Well, how else would he call? Oh, sorry, Nita, I'm not mad at *you*." Anne bounced up in bed and the orange fairy-tale book fell on the floor. "You should've seen Petrova dancing around, saying, 'Annie has a boyfriend, Annie has a boyfriend.' And Dad laughed! I hate them. And anyway, Henry's *your* stupid prince."

"He is not. Oh, you mean in the play," said Nita. "Why did he call?" Henry was a thing that happened in school, not a person who called you on the phone.

"His mother wants to measure for our costumes. She's going to come to school tomorrow."

Nita's worlds shifted around a little more. Now there was a new world called "Henry's house." "Where is it? I mean, where does he live?"

"You know the vegetable stand on the road to Maushope? In there. They've got a farm, and Dad says they're the last of their kind. Maybe that's good, considering they've got Henry."

"Do they grow mangoes?"

"I don't think mangoes grow in Massachusetts."

By this time, Nita had on her pajamas and her bed was all arranged: stuffed cat, two pillows. She went to brush her teeth, then hurried back and jumped under the covers.

From the attic came a series of lonely, haunting cries.

"The owls are calling," said Anne. Nita imagined the owls soaring in the dark night over the Landing, their soft feathers protecting them from the cold, their sharp eyes seeing everything.

Anne turned out the light. The black shadows of the night took over the bedroom, and Nita drifted off.

Seventeen

THE NEXT DAY, Nita tried to look up owls in her book about Thailand, but the word *owl* was not in the index. She couldn't find *birds* either. But she still felt a strange sense of already knowing some of the things in the book. She remembered more and more Thai words and was copying some of them out of the book for her report when Brenda came back into the classroom and said, "Hey, Nita, I think I saw your Dad."

Nita shot out of her chair. "Where?"

"In his car, out front."

Mrs. Sommers looked at the girls with a question in her eyes.

"Can I go see if my Dad is out there?" Nita asked softly. The teacher nodded.

Nita flew down the old wooden stairs and out into the playground. He was there! She raced down the walk and hopped into the passenger side of Dad's old blue car. He hugged her hard with one arm. "Oh, Daddy, you came back."

"Hey, I wasn't gone that long. Do you think your teacher will spring you a little early?"

"Six days *is* long," said Nita, but she ran back to ask Mrs. Sommers and get her coat. Dad's coming home felt like snow in July or a surprise party. Like the owl, he just flew into her world and made it seem so different. "Where are we going?" she asked as she got back in the car.

"I thought we'd go out to our house and see the new construction you and Pudge got going while I was out of your hair."

Was he pleased? Nita couldn't tell. "Did he tell you about the Roots Committee?"

"Yes, and he told me about some other things, too. Seems like you've been very busy while I've been gone."

They drove along Water Street and turned down toward the beach. Nita wondered if he knew Bill was angry at him.

As they got closer to their house, they could see the

new window bulging out of the white side wall. A man on a ladder was painting the trim.

"Hi, Frank," said Nita's dad.

"Hello, Lieutenant Orson, sir," said Frank.

Inside, the whole kitchen was torn up. Nita stumbled over some cans of paint.

"Putting in that window turned out to be more complicated than Pudge thought," said Dad. "They found some water damage in the walls. Then they decided to paint the kitchen and the living room while they're at it."

Nita felt confused. This is what you wanted, isn't it? she said to herself. For Dad to come home, for us all to come home. But now, even if they all did come home, it would be different. Better? Or just different? And it smelled funny because of the paint, so it seemed even less like home than when she had been there with Petrova.

Dad was looking kind of unhappy, too, not the way he had when he first picked her up. "So, we can't stay here. I guess I'll stay down at the base and you can stay with the Stillwaters' for a few more days. Marian says it's fine, she loves having you. Okay, kiddo?"

"No, it's not okay," said Nita.

Dad looked at her in surprise.

"I mean, I thought Mom could come home when you got here. I thought . . ." She couldn't go on.

"I'll go see her tonight." Dad had his old worried look again.

"She talked to me. She *is* better," said Nita firmly, as if this would make it true.

"I know. They told me on the phone, but she can't come home just yet. You have to be patient, Nita. We want her to get *really* better. We don't want her to slip back again."

Nita tried to smile.

"That's my girl," said Dad. "I tell you what. Let's go get a cup of coffee, I mean, some ice cream or something. I'll tell you about the cruise." Nita leaned against Dad in the car and pretended he had never been away and that Mom was waiting for them at home.

They stopped at the Docksider on Water Street.

Nita sat down at the sunniest table and said, "I'll have a banana split."

"I thought you hated your flavors all mixed up." Dad looked surprised.

"I did? I guess I'm different now," said Nita slowly. When her banana split arrived, in a dish shaped like a boat, she took a bite each of the chocolate ice cream with marshmallow sauce, the strawberry ice cream with pineapple sauce, and the vanilla ice cream with chocolate sauce. Then she took a bite of banana. Dad had coffee and mud pie while he told her about the new navigation system of the *Islandia*. Then he said, "So what have you been doing?"

"Well," she said, "Petrova and I banded the snowy owl. Remember the snowy owl I told you about? We used my earmuffs for bait and the owl thought they were a rabbit! So he swooped down and we caught him. Petrova had this great trap that doesn't really hurt the owls, it just . . ."

Nita went on and on with her story until Dad finally said, "Whoa, slow down, I've never heard you talk so much in your whole life." But he laughed as he spoke, so Nita could see he really *liked* having her go on and on this way.

She kept talking to keep Dad listening, but finally even her enormous banana split was finished. Dad paid the bill, and when they came out of the restaurant, they walked up and down the street looking in windows, as if they were on vacation or it was a holiday.

And then Nita saw it again. The sun quilt. It glowed in the afternoon light and lit up the whole street. A huge burst of color, made of hundreds of tiny scraps. "Look!" breathed Nita. It was even more wonderful than the first time she saw it. Dad stopped in his tracks.

"That's amazing," he said. "Each scrap is separate, and yet they make a pattern."

The quilt glowed in the late afternoon light like a thousand hummingbirds, like a multicolored sun.

"Maybe . . . maybe," said Nita, "we could buy it for Ma-jah."

"Oh, it's probably much too expensive. And why are you calling her Ma-jah?"

"Because I'm going to speak Thai to her. You know about the Roots Committee."

"If only she hadn't taken that trip ho—back to Thailand."

"See, you almost said 'trip *home*'! Oh, Dad, let's just *ask* about the quilt. If we put it on her bed, then it won't be white like a freezing snow bank, but a promise of the sun coming back. Maybe then she'll remember that if she feels bad, she could get better, the way the days get longer and the winter ends and the sun gets warmer. Then she'll *like* being home."

Dad looked at her. "Well, you're . . . maybe this acting . . . honestly, Nita, I've never heard you talk like that before. But"—he held up his hands—"I get your drift." He opened the shop door.

"It's expensive," said Dad, looking at the back of the quilt and fingering the tag. Then he peered around to see the front of it again.

"Everything here is handmade," said the woman at the counter.

Nita held her breath and just looked at Dad, silently pleading, almost begging him. Please? said her eyes.

"Aye, aye, sir! Let's do it!" said Dad, laughing at Nita's spaniel look.

"A wonderful present," said the salesperson. She took Dad's check. "Thank you very much."

Nita beamed at her. "Thank *you*, and could you tell the person who made it how much we like it?"

"It was a group of people, actually, in a handicapped workshop." She smiled back at Nita. "They're up in Maushop and they always make such beautiful things, I just—"

"Thanks. Good-bye," said Dad, as if he were a bit tired of all this chatting. So who's impatient now, thought Nita.

"What a great idea, Nita," he said, squeezing her arm as they walked back out onto Water Street. "She'll love it. For the first time, I feel like she really will come home."

Nita smiled back at him. Now, she thought, maybe he will stay home, too.

Eighteen

DAD STAYED in Maushope's Landing, but he didn't go home, and Nita couldn't either. Wednesday Dad came to the Stillwaters' for dinner, and Thursday he took them all out for Chinese food. Still, no one said when Ma-jah could come home, but Nita was so busy with rehearsals, she only had a few minutes to think each night before she fell asleep. Then she would see the lighthouse flashing in her mind's eye and think, Home, home! before she drowsed off.

On Friday morning, nothing seemed to go right.

"Has anyone seen my Thailand report?" asked Nita. The Stillwater breakfast table was covered with cereal bowls, geology journals, yesterday's mail, and one red mitten, but no Thailand report appeared in the jumble.

"I can't find my Thailand report," said Nita. She searched in her school bag and knocked over the jam.

"Your report's in the fruit bowl under the bananas, of course," said Petrova. "Hey, we glued your coffin together again yesterday. I hear you wrecked it the first time, so could you *please* be more careful?"

Mrs. S. looked at Nita. "Your coffin?"

"For the play," muttered Nita. She found her report in the fruit bowl and headed out of there before anyone could ask another question.

All week, she'd managed to forget the last act of the play when she had to get in that damned, yes *damned*, coffin. Just calling it that made her feel a little bit better, but at the rehearsal, when David and the dwarfs carried it in from the back porch of the school, Nita shivered. An actual cold shudder ran up her spine.

"Three of us on each side and one for her head," said the dwarf Pokey.

"I don't think I can," said Nita, and her heart thumped.

"Yes, get in," said Sleepy. "I'd love to get in there and snore."

"But drop it very carefully, guys," said Amy.

"*Very* carefully," said David, "or the sides will fall off, and that will look ridiculous."

"I really don't want to," said Nita.

"You have to. And you have to be dropped. Otherwise, how will the poison apple get unstuck from your throat? Trust us, Nita," said Amy. Her brown eyes were serious.

It was hard to say no to Amy.

Nita couldn't believe she was doing it, but once more she got into the plastic box and let them close the lid. She took a deep breath and shut her eyes. And like a vision, the snowy owl, soaring over the beach, sprang into her waiting mind. Her breathing slowed down and she rested.

A loud whisper made her eyes fly open. Henry knelt by the coffin and practically spit his words through the air holes. "Oh, Princess S. W.," he slobbered, "I cannot live without you."

No one heard him but Nita.

"Speak up, Henry," said Amy. "Throw your voice to the back of the room."

Henry stood up and stomped off the stage. This time he galloped in, as if he were on a prancing horse. He waved his sword toward the coffin. "I must have her," he shouted. "Get going, dwarfs, and carry her to my castle."

Nita lay in the plastic coffin. Through the plastic she could see Henry waving his sword. It looked like a crazy world out there with Henrys in it. Right now, I don't mind it in here. At least I'm protected from the spit.

"Time out," called Amy. Her words came faintly to Nita.

Saved! David opened the coffin and Nita sat up to see what had called a halt to the action. Sounds got louder and there was a bustle around the door.

"Ma!" said Henry. He tripped over his sword as he headed toward a large pile of clothes that was moving into the room on two little legs. "Is that you, Ma?"

"In here," said a muffled voice from the pile of clothes. The clothes landed on a desk, and Mrs. Sporoni rubbed her back. "There now. Costumes. Dwarf jackets and a fabulous skirt for you, Anita, if I do say so myself." Mrs. Sporoni beamed at Nita, even if she didn't get her name right, and brought the fabulous skirt over to her. It was embroidered with white flowers that had embroidered holes. You could see the pale pink underskirt through the cutwork.

Nita fingered the fabric shyly. "Did you do all that fancy sewing?" she asked.

"Lord, no," said Mrs. Sporoni. "It's my old tablecloth. Doesn't it look great? Get out of your coffin, lovey, and I'll slip it over your head."

The waist fit perfectly and the silk underskirt rustled when Nita walked. Maybe being in the play wouldn't be so bad, wearing this dress. On the other hand, she could see how it was: they dress you all up in pretty clothes and then you have to marry Henry. She would have to read more of Anne's fairy-tale books to see if there was a way out of this destiny.

"Roll up your jeans," said Anne. "What a great skirt. But you can't wear sneakers. You can borrow my pink ballet shoes if you like."

"You guys look pretty girlie," said Henry to Nita and Brenda, who was posing in slinky black silk.

His mother squelched him with a glance. "Get your homework together, Prince Henry," she ordered. "My coach won't wait."

Henry went off as meek as a lamb. Brenda stabbed her long fingernails in the direction of his retreating back in a witch's hex.

"See, that wasn't so bad, was it, Nita?" said Amy with a grin. "I guess you've put off the carrying until next week. Last rehearsals next week, guys! See you then." She pulled on her jacket.

Suddenly, the play seemed awfully real. Am I really going to get up there in front of all those people? Don't think about it, Nita told herself fiercely, you'll just scare yourself to death, and then you *will* need a coffin.

"Anne," she said, "will you walk down to the base with me? Dad's going to take me to see Mom and he'll give you a ride home."

"Sure, and we could take the long-cut and go see the pigeons."

They put all the clothes away carefully and went out into the darkening afternoon. The sky was streaked with red over the harbor and the water was a steely dark blue. Nita took a deep breath of the chilly air as she watched the red winter sun slip below the horizon.

Nineteen

WHEN THE TWO girls reached the parking lot, one plain dark gray bird with a tiny head balanced on the railing of the bridge, its outline etched against the sunset exactly like a shadow puppet.

Another pigeon flapped up under the bridge and several others bobbed along the pavement. A pink-green-purple sheen livened up their dark gray necks, like an oil slick on a rain puddle.

"Why did the story say 'but at last came the dove'?" Anne wondered. "I mean, why '*but* at last,' as if some great thing was going to happen?"

"Well, some great thing *did* happen. Ma-jah talked! It means the bemoaning worked! Snow White woke up, Ma-jah talked. It was like . . . like going back to normal life."

"Look! That pigeon's got a little stick," said Anne. "Do you think it's making a nest? In January?" They watched the heavy bird flap up under the bridge.

"I think it means Ma-jah's coming home, back to *our* nest," said Nita.

"Petrova would say it's just a coincidence," said Anne. "But, I hope it's true."

They left the pigeons and found Dad just coming out of the main Coast Guard building. "Hi, Anne. Hi, Nita," he said. "Do you want to eat supper here? They're having meat loaf." Dad knew Nita loved Coast Guard meat loaf.

"Can I call my parents?" asked Anne. Good smells drifted down the hall. Nita sniffed hungrily as Anne dialed home from the petty officer's desk.

The dining room was like a little restaurant, all brown and shiny. They got their trays and found a table in the corner, where Nita's red sweatshirt stood out among all the dark blue uniforms. There was a clatter of dishes, and people smiled to see Dad with her and Anne. It was cozy at the Coast Guard base, like living in the woods with the dwarfs. Dad looked like he wished he could stay right here forever. Nita could see why.

Captain Pudge came by and beamed at them. "That window's just about finished," he said.

Dad smiled back. "Great! We really want to move back in this weekend."

"Yay!" said Nita. "How about tomorrow?" She grabbed Dad's hand and squeezed it. "I love your meat loaf, Captain P—uh, Vanderpost."

He patted his round stomach. "So do I," he said, "made it myself, that's the only way to get what you want around here!" The men at the next table burst out laughing.

Dad pushed back his chair. "Let's go, girls," he said. "We've got to get to the hospital." He bussed his tray and waved good-bye to his buddies. Nita gulped down her milk, and the girls hurried after him.

After they dropped off Anne, the problem that had been nagging away at Nita came back to her.

"Dad, why does Snow White have to marry Prince Henry? I mean, he's kind of weird. Even when he thought she was dead, he wanted to keep her at his castle like something in a museum."

"It's only a story," said Dad, as he pulled into the visitors' parking lot.

"It's like how you want Mom to stay in the lighthouse while you go to sea, or out with your dwar—Coast Guard buddies."

Dad stopped the car. "Is *that* what you think?" He gave Nita an intense look out of his blue eyes. Then he rubbed his forehead. "Maybe you're right. I like knowing you guys are there, my beautiful princesses in our lighthouse tower." He smiled.

Maybe I can talk to Mom—Ma-jah—about the prince problem, thought Nita. Dad doesn't understand.

"Dad says it's only a story, but why does the story have to be like that?" asked Nita later.

Once more, Ma-jah was in her chair and Nita was curled up on Ma-jah's bed. Dad had gone to talk to the doctor.

"Just because the apple gets unstuck from her throat when the dwarfs drop her, it doesn't mean she has to get married," Nita argued. "Just because the Prince wants to marry her doesn't mean she wants to marry *him*."

Ma-jah smiled. "Maybe she is grateful to the prince who has saved her from the demon owl."

Boy, she still didn't like owls. "Even in Thailand, it always has to be the prince?"

"Oh, yes," said Ma-jah.

"And was Dad your prince?"

"Oh, yes," said Ma-jah. "He saved me. My family was afraid we would lose the farm. It was just like a story—of the rich neighbor and the poor mango farmer. My family wanted me to marry the son of the rich neighbor, but I didn't like him."

"They *did*?" Nita could not imagine Ma-jah married to anyone but Dad.

"But then," said Ma-jah, "I met your father and went to America with him."

"What about the farm?"

"My sister married the son of the rich neighbor. Remember, we visited the farm when you were little?"

"Yes, I remember! Where there were lizards."

"Jing-jok," said Ma-jah. "I'm glad you remember." A faint smile lingered on her face. Nita loved watching it. I never knew all those things about Ma-jah, she thought. Parents are like opening a book in the middle, a book that has all those chapters before you were born.

"Did your sister like the rich farmer's son?"

"I think so." Ma-jah closed her eyes.

Nita tiptoed out of the room. "She talks more and more every time, doesn't she?" she said to Dad in the hallway.

As they headed out to the car, she asked, "When can she come home?"

"I'm going to talk to the doctor again tomorrow," said Dad.

"Next week's the play," said Nita.

"Nita, I really don't want you to count on Mom coming to the play. The noise, the crowd—it will all be too much for her, I'm afraid. But I'll be there, with bells on."

"Bells?" Nita looked at him, imagining him in a jester hat or as a horse with a sleigh-bell harness. Why was he talking about stupid bells, when Mom wasn't even going to come to her play?

"Not real bells," he said. "It means, I'm looking forward to it." He took a deep breath and added, "And I'm looking forward to moving back to our castle tomorrow. I'll come and get you first thing." The car stopped in front of the Stillwaters' house.

Nita threw her arms around Dad's neck and kissed him on the cheek. "I'll get up early! Good night, Dad."

One minute she felt so angry because he didn't understand *anything* and the next minute she loved him again. More opposite things, thought Nita, as she got out in the cold and ran inside the house.

Twenty

NITA AND DAD spent Saturday morning unpacking clothes, watering orchids, arranging the quilt on the bed, and buying groceries.

"We've got to have something besides eggs," said Nita. "Maybe I could learn to make the Captain's meat loaf."

"I bet you could," said Dad as he lugged the big bag of birdseed out to the feeder.

Nita called Captain Pudge at the base and got his recipe, or at least what he *said* was his recipe. It started: first, catch a cow. Maybe they'd just eat the hamburger they'd already bought.

The new window looked really good, and they

arranged all the orchids on the built-in shelves. The little mouths on the orchids didn't say any mean things to Nita this morning.

It was so great to be home that Nita didn't miss Mom as much as she thought she would. Getting things ready for her was almost as good as her being there.

Nita watched out the window for the owls as she worked. She thought she saw one lift off far down the beach. Dad got a glimpse of the white bird, too, and Nita hoped they wouldn't go away.

"Dad, can you help me with my Thailand report? I forgot to bring home my library book," said Nita.

"I don't know how much you want to know about the Coast Guard Loran station," he said. "But I can tell you a little bit about growing mangoes."

By Sunday night, the house was ready. Now Mom's place really seemed empty, but Nita didn't want to worry Dad by talking about it. She was glad when Monday came, with school and rehearsals. Even the dread report was shaping up.

The class worked so hard rehearsing and creating the set for the first four days of that week that Mrs. Sommers called them the "Famous Amy Bradley Two-Week Special." "You should hire yourself out," said Mrs. Sommers to Amy on Friday afternoon. "I really didn't think you could do this in two weeks, but you've proved me wrong." They stood in the kindergarten room and admired the dwarfs' house, the Huntsman's costume, complete with ax, and the cutout birds that Anne and Nita were arranging on a tree branch in what was usually the flag holder.

"It's because we make the script just like an outline," said Amy. "You don't have to memorize."

"I don't know why it is," said Mrs. Sommers. "But I think it's magic."

As Nita looked around the kindergarten room, it did seem like magic. A fairy-tale world had appeared right there in the old wood-paneled schoolroom.

"And tonight's the showdown!" shouted Henry.

"You mean the performance," said Amy. "We're almost there."

"Two hours, forty-five minutes, and twenty-nine seconds," said Nita. She knew exactly the amount of time she had left until she had to get up in front of all those people.

Twenty-one

T H A T   E V E N I N G, as Nita came in from
the cold, dark outside, she didn't look at
the stage, but hurried into the first-grade room,
which was the dressing room. She took off her ski
jacket and uncovered Anne's white angora sweater,
which she wore over the skirt Henry's mother
had fixed for her. A makeup mother rushed over,
painted her mouth with red lipstick, and combed her
black hair.

"There you go," said the makeup mother. "White as
snow, black as ebony, and red as blood. Perfect."

The kindergarten room looked like a real theater. A
tentlike blue canopy covered the back of the platform.

Stars shone on the blue, making a glittering backdrop for the action on stage. A black tree with twisted branches loomed overhead; when the Mirror danced in, it had exactly the same kind of twisted wood for a frame.

Nita felt she was sliding into a dream. Now that she had on her costume, she *was* Snow White. As she drifted around the room, no one spoke to her. They could see she was in the play already, and they couldn't talk to her because they weren't there yet.

Acting is so great, Nita thought. You can be anyone— a princess, a deep-sea diver, probably you could even *fly*. That would be nice.

Henry brought her down to earth. "Hey, Nita," he said, "Want to see something?"

If I didn't know him, thought Nita, I might even think he was handsome. Henry wore a blue velvet jacket, jodhpurs, and boots.

"You're the one who likes birds so much. Want to see something?" he repeated.

"I guess so," she said cautiously.

Henry pulled a tattered photo out of his pocket. "This is a really good bird. He oughta be in this play, because he can *talk*!"

Nita looked at the gray parrot with red tail feathers. It was a nice-looking parrot, but what really caught her attention was the boy with the Asian face who held the parrot on his arm. "Who's that?" she asked.

"Oh, that's my friend Paul, he only comes here in the summer. But that's his great parrot, Sultry, that can *talk*. He says 'Birds don't talk.' Get it? His *bird* says 'Birds don't talk.' Get it?"

"I get it. What else does he say?"

"He makes a sound like a bomb dropping, and a sound like water filling up, *glug-glug-glug,* and he sings 'When it's springtime in the Rockies.' "

But Nita was studying the face that looked like hers in the photo. "Do you tell Paul he looks like a monkey?" she asked.

"Sure. I call him 'monk' and he calls me 'klutz' because I'm always tripping over things. Now I've gotta go get my sword. See ya!" Henry grinned and ran off.

I'll *never* understand Henry, thought Nita.

Voices rose louder and louder. The audience was arriving in the kindergarten room.

Dwarfs were everywhere. Brown jackets and red caps wove in and out of the crowded dressing room and hall. Nita smiled when she saw Bill Stillwater struggling through a bunch of dwarfs to get to his seat.

"Heigh ho, heigh ho, it's time to start the show," sang Anne. She danced around Nita.

Brenda was not smiling. "This stupid fingernail," she

hissed. "It broke! I glued it back together with Super Glue and it better not break again."

"Quiet, please," said Amy. "Five minutes to curtain."

Two dwarfs got ready to pull the front panels of starry blue fabric to the sides of the room and loop them up so the audience could see the Queen's bedroom. Later Snow White would be lost in the woods in front of the curtains, and the dwarfs' house would be set up where the Queen's bedroom was now.

The audience quieted down. Anne and the dwarf named Silly went through the hall to the kindergarten room. "Tonight we would like to present to you *Snow White and the Dwarfs*," came Anne's high, clear voice.

When Nita heard Brenda's first lines they seemed to come from far, far away. Then Snow White was out in the dark woods with the Huntsman.

The play went without a hitch. Nita was so far into her part that she didn't even feel afraid when the dwarfs lifted her into the coffin. Her body felt lifeless.

She lay in the coffin and watched the bird shadows above her. The cutout owl, raven, and dove made by the props committee seemed alive. Their shadows quivered on the wall and the dwarfs wailed in sorrow, bemoaning. Nita closed her eyes. She heard Henry's voice. She felt the coffin shift, then lift, and she bumped around a little as the dwarfs stomped around singing.

Finally, Snow White was sprung from her deathlike sleep by the bumping of the coffin, which shook loose the poison apple. Prince Henry yanked her hand so she nearly fell over as he tried to help her out of the plastic box, but she kept her balance, and the spotlights burst with light as she rose to her feet. The audience applauded madly. Nita felt dazed, like an astronaut suddenly arriving home from outer space.

"Heigh ho, heigh ho, it's off to church we go," sang the dwarfs. And so Snow White married the Prince. The audience clapped again.

They cheered when the Queen tap-danced in her red tap shoes as red crepe-paper flames of hell burned and waved around her.

Under cover of the clapping and cheering, Nita jerked her hand out of Henry's. "Now I'm going back to live in the woods with the dwarfs," Nita told him.

"Yes, let's," he answered. "That'll be awesome."

"Not *you*. You have to go back to your castle."

"What?" bellowed Henry. The applause was very loud. He grinned at Nita. It was too noisy to make him understand.

When they were on their third curtain call, Henry grabbed Nita's hand again and dragged her out of the row of actors to take a special bow just for the two of them.

There was Dad, and there was Captain Pudge, and, could it really be? There was Mom! Suddenly Nita felt her flying feeling, as if she had lifted off and floated over the audience for just a minute. Then the applause ended and the audience crowded up around the actors.

Nita pushed through the crowd and hugged her mother tight, forgetting that she was fragile and not strong. Ma-jah hugged her back and laughed. "Why didn't you say you were coming?" said Nita. "Why didn't you *tell* me?"

Dad answered. "We hoped, but we didn't want to disappoint you, Nita." He put one arm around Mom and one around Nita and squeezed.

Ma-jah smiled. "It gave me something to look forward to," she murmured in Nita's ear.

Mrs. S. rushed over and kissed Nita's cheek. "I had no idea you could act like that," she said, looking at Nita with pride, as if somehow she belonged a little bit to her. "You're such a small person, but large and amazing on the stage."

Captain Pudge gave her a thumbs-up sign, and then Dad waved his camera. "Let's get a good shot now," he said. "Even I believed you were Snow White for a while there, kiddo. Get over here, Henry!"

Nita looked around and saw all her classmates and their parents. "The play was great," she said. "The sets were terrific, and acting is fun. Everything is wonderful!" She whirled around and punched Henry in the shoulder. "Even *you* are not so bad," she said.

Henry laughed. This was the kind of joke he could understand. He ran into the back hall and hung on the bell rope. *Clang, clang! Clang, clang!* The news of their triumph sounded out in the frosty air of Maushope's Landing.

Twenty-two

A FEW DAYS later, Nita pressed her face against the window and cupped her hands by her eyes to shield them from the late afternoon sun. Two blue jays squabbled on the bird feeder and the driveway glistened where the brownish snow melted and ran down in a tiny river.

Behind Nita, Ma-jah stirred something on the stove. "Maybe he's gone north," said Ma-jah. "With this January thaw, it'll be too warm for him here."

"I wanted you to see him," said Nita. She had been searching the sky every day this week. "I wanted you to see him, so you can see he is a good spirit."

"Suppose you were a mouse," said Ma-jah. "Then

what would you think?" But she smiled as she said this. Since she had come back to her newly painted living room, the orchid window, which flooded the room with light, and her glowing sun quilt, Ma-jah's spirits seemed to be rekindled.

A painting by Anne of the two quarreling children that looked like her and Petrova hung up on the wall. It was Anne's contribution to the Roots Committee. Nita's Thailand report lay on the table, marked with a red A-.

Nita still worried. True, the snow had thawed, but there was February to come, with more snow and ice, more dark and cold. Nita searched the curve of the beach, the dunes and the sky. A bank of fog was creeping in across the water from the east. Soon the afternoon would be over. If she could see the owl one more time, and if Ma-jah could see it . . .

"Look!" she shouted. "Come quick!" She almost couldn't believe it, but, yes, there was the flash of white on the beach.

Ma-jah ran to the window. "Oh, Nita," she murmured, "you were right. When I was sick it seemed I was in a long, dark tunnel, until one day, I saw a tiny speck of light at the end. But maybe it wasn't daylight, maybe it was your beautiful owl."

Nita and her mother watched as the white owl

soared over the beach, catching the last rays of the sun.

Then the big light came on in the lighthouse next door. Flash! And then dark. Flash! And then dark.

The foghorn moaned; it had a safe, comforting sound. The owl was gone.